RELATIVES

IN

I0534448

COMMON

M. VonEmbs

www.relativesincommon.com

The story:

For some folks life is pretty easy, for others it is a disaster from their first breath in this world, each and every day until their last. Will you hate the man as much as you pity the childhood which created him? Can you forgive as easy as you can condemn? Southern Ohio offers a little bit of everything and a whole lot of nothing, it's always been this way, I can't imagine it'll change. You never know who you may be related to.

The term: **FBI** as it is used in this book stands for the: Fun But Intrusive organization, and has nothing whatsoever to do with the prestigious and always respected secretive US government organization that coincidentally shares the same abbreviation.

The cursing, racial remarks, misspellings, slang words are all part of the story and do not reflect the author's true sentiment in any way.

Chapters

Chapter 1, Chicago 2009

April 20, 2009

FBI Director:

This Southern Ohio case was on the stone cold stack for 30 years, and remains unsolved after 50 years. We've recently found a person of interest in Chicago. She's elderly and from what we already know, more than half nuts. Hit it up, see what's there.

FBI Agent:

We're on it.

May 1, 2009 Chicago, Illinois

Knock knock, Mrs. Hoffmiller? . . . . . . Knock knock knock, Mrs. Violet Hoffmiller? We are investigating a crime Mrs. Hoffmiller, we need to ask you a few questions…We are federal agent's madam, we need to speak with you Mrs. Hoffmiller.

Slowly the door opens and a small woman with a feather boa stole and dark horn brimmed sunglasses stands in the doorway. Everything was white and the lights were so bright that the agents could barely see.

Yes, I am Mrs. Hoffmiller, do come in.

Mrs. Hoffmiller did you live in Hillsboro, Ohio with a Bernard Hoffmiller between the years of 1948 until around 1952 and 1953?

Unfortunately yes, yes I did.

Also, can you dim the lights madam and turn off the source of that noise?

A loud angry voice responds: Ohhh no . . . , NO I will NOT! This is my art and my art will not be disrespected in any way!

The agents looked at each other, raised their eyebrows and shrugged their shoulders.

The old woman was screaming at federal agents and refusing to dim the lights. This was turning out to be quite a day. . .

-Fade to white -

Diana

Sixty seven and one-half years earlier in the fall of 1942 as the war raged in Europe, thousands of miles away outside of Waverly, Ohio a smaller battle that few would ever know about was underway. Diana Smith was ready to give birth to twins.

Diana, who routinely had the hell beat out of her by the father of the children she was about to deliver, had driven herself over fifty miles in a beat up old car trying to get to a preacher who also claimed to be a doctor. She was beyond pitiful, with two black eyes and a swollen face.

Things were not good for Diana, they never had been.

Her life to this point had been brutal. Her father had lost his life in a mine explosion. Soon after her father died, her mother lost her mind and then her children. Diana was a little slow, at least that's what they called it at the time. She had been shuffled through many foster homes, including a few that would remain forever guilty of horrific crimes. Raped, sodomized and passed on. Orphaned children were always at the top of the vulnerable list.

If the emotional strain of not having a real family wasn't painful enough, the fear of what a foster parent may do to you never left your mind. For Diana the holidays had always been the most difficult, without even an aunt and uncle to claim you.

There was a snide pecking order among the orphans. The kids that were occasionally claimed by relatives flaunted it whenever they could. Many of the children had absolutely no one.

Some of these children would create elaborate tales regarding their parentless status, easing the pain of being completely abandoned and left to the state.

From killing tigers in India to fighting in unknown wars, the reasons for their abandonment could be quite vivid, always avoiding the most obvious fact that no one wanted them.

They were frequently made fun of by the other children. . . *Your mommy is the State of Ohio, but your daddy didn't dick'er, spose'n your daddy is Governor John Bricker.*

Life was incredibly harsh for these children of the state in the 1930s, it seems harshness always finds its way to those who least deserve it.

Out of guilt or for more sinister reasons, many families would take in orphaned children just for the holidays. Being a "holiday take in," you would unknowingly carry around an uneasy vacant expression of not belonging where you were, often ending up in a new home a few days or maybe a week before Christmas, usually whisked out before New Year's. This nervous unease was so easily misconstrued as being ungrateful.

While the real children of the household were excited thinking about the arrival of Santa Claus and the wonderful presents they would receive, your only Christmas hope was to avoid a late night visit from their father in your makeshift attic or basement bedroom a million miles away from Bing Crosby's soothing voice, or the festive house, where your choices would be presented in the starkest of terms.

Sick minds got away with it then, sometimes prominent men in the community and their often silent but equally guilty wives. At that time almost everyone had heard rumors about someone or had a "special" uncle, cousin or neighbor that you dare not be alone with, set on their lap or god forbid spend the night at their home.

There were no children's rights, no women's rights, and no DNA testing, just one word against another, continual molestation and rape after rape.

Male perpetrators were protected by male police officers, forgiven by male clergy, treated by male doctors, governed by male congressmen and male senators, tried in court by male judges, and represented by male lawyers. Guilty or innocent, they were nearly always welcomed home by their protective wives, the mothers of their legitimate families.

Even a woman with some prestige and influence would've had a difficult time. A woman or young woman with a "reputation," even a fabricated one, would never climb the hurdle of "force without consent."

In those days consent was nearly granted by just your presence, your innocence stripped away just as rapidly and easily as your dress.

Ignorant phrases like: "well, she just shouldn't have been there" or "she was just in the wrong place at the wrong time" were quite common and simply accepted justifications of a potentially horrific crime.

If you ended up criminally pregnant, you would give birth to a bastard that you became solely responsible for. Society has now deemed you to be no more than a warm catch basin for the uninvited fertilization of one of your body's most precious functions.

You shall receive what has been given.

The word: BASTARD, forever printed on your child's birth certificate. You were now the proud raped mother of a bastard. If you were a girl or young woman, you would be forced to give the child up for adoption.

The nuns would snatch your baby before it had taken its first breath, and then fill you full of lies while holding your hand, frantically praying for your forgiveness. If you were a bit older you could give the child up or take on the very difficult task of trying to raise it on your own with little to no help from anyone.

A fatherless child could only mean that you were a whore, perhaps a raped whore but a whore nonetheless.

In order to stay off the "beg," you will now live in a strange town, lie about where you came from, wear the wedding band of your imaginary dead husband, and forever work twice as hard for one fourth of the money.
If that's not enough, young widows, even fake ones, were easy pickings. There was no expectation of fairness and seldom a glimpse of it.

Ravished so completely, discarded with contempt.

Diana never wore the type of clothes or shoes the other kids wore; her clothes were always musty and stained. Her dresses looked like they were thrown on the floor wet and allowed to dry in a wrinkled heap. Her shoes were older ladies styled and noticeably second-hand.

It was obvious that she had never been taught to care for herself. She did not understand why the other children ignored her.

Diana had her first period near the end of the fifth grade. She thought she was bleeding to death and she had no idea what was happening to her. She ran wailing through the halls of the school crying for anyone to help her. A hoard of children followed her through the halls, all laughing and pointing. Diana begged as the group of onlookers had tightened around her. Her stinking tattered dress was fully soaked with menstrual and the school children were screaming horrible things to her. All of them chanting ignorance to a little girl who needed help so badly. Diana needed just one friend in this world, one small hand to reach out to her, but it wasn't to be.

Not even a teacher paid much attention to what was going on. Finally Diana was taken aside, scrubbed up and made to return to class stains and all.

Cruelty couldn't begin to describe these children. Just like their church going and very forgiven parents, distributing fresh gossip and assigning personal blame were always more important than extending a hand.

It was obvious that the forgiven had no interest whatsoever in forgiving. These people were the masters of telling you how good they were, all while subtlety reminding you of the various reasons that you were doomed to hell while they would be high above you in heaven, still looking down on you, still calling you names supposedly with Jesus at their side.

While it was very well-known in the community that Diana needed help, she was easily overlooked and she would not be chosen.

The charities of the local well-to-do and faux well-to-do were carefully selected for the sole purpose of economy and easy promotion.

Helping one obviously abused and desperate little girl would not fill their hearts nearly as much as the over publicized fake letters of thanks written in perfect English from a family in a faraway land that could be fed for pennies without really doing a dammed thing.

Half way through her sixth grade Diana became pregnant from her latest foster father, Mr. Eldon Simpson.

Mr. Simpson had repeatedly raped Diana from the day she moved in six months earlier.

His manicured lawn and perfect exterior façade concealed his activities completely.

Mr. Simpson was a clean-cut, God fearing man. In fact, he was one of the tidiest most organized men you could ever meet.

His appearance, car, yard and home were spotless and perfect. He never drank, didn't smoke and had a stellar work record. He was a respected man in the community.

There was just one thing wrong with Mr. Eldon Simpson, he was a devious child raping pedophile.

His crimes so easily facilitated by a lax system of trial adoption that never considered the wellbeing of a child. Placement was the word of the day with little concern for what you were being placed in.

Once a young lady was labeled "troubled," her fate was sealed for the likes of Mr. Simpson. He and his wife had taken in many "troubled" girls in the past, all between the ages of twelve and fifteen, all early bloomers, all carefully selected for one insidious purpose. Each of them had run away, not one had ever returned.

For Mr. Simpson, Diana's young body was like a fresh bottle for a perpetual drunk.

His wife always knew what was happening, she knew that her husband was a horrible and disgusting man, yet she did nothing because just like all of the others before, Diana was just a lying little whore who deserved whatever came her way in this life. She completely disregarded what she knew was occurring, never making eye contact with Diana.

Through the years, no one had ever questioned Eldon's horrible acts or his wife's silent consent, not once. Only his victims knew the truth and they were all worthless transient whores who had only served to replenish the system for future versions of Mr. Simpson with his own offspring.

These people in this part of Ohio and at this time in America seemed completely at odds with the patriotic reality that was slowly gripping the rest of the country as the threat of war loomed.

Eldon and his wife thought of Diana not as a young girl or even a fellow human being, but as a needy object who didn't deserve the respect of their dog. They had long ago lost the ability to take pity on anyone other than themselves.

Diana really just wanted someone, anyone to care about her because no one ever had from the time she was born. She didn't realize or care that she had the body of a woman much earlier than most; she didn't realize the curse it was. Enduring the brutal acts perpetrated by Eldon had somehow become worth the attention that accompanied it; it was after all the only affection she received from anyone. Sexual violation felt natural to Diana, and to her this was normal. Giving herself to a man had become no different than changing socks. It had evolved into something that was routine, expected and quite mechanical.

She had no concept of right and wrong with regards to her body. No one had ever told Diana what she shouldn't do, in fact only what she should do when stripped naked and ravaged by a fellow human being with no conscience and no morals. But every Sunday morning as the bells of forgiveness rang and without one hair out of place, the Lord forgave Eldon for his brutality, and every other night of the week he raped the current young lady he and his wife had been entrusted to care for. This had been going on for many years.

Recently Eldon had skipped a week of services in protest. He was furious that the church had overlooked printing his name in the monthly circular, thanking him in bold letters for making a two hundred dollar donation to their remodeling efforts.

It didn't matter; Jesus would be patiently waiting next Sunday for Eldon, always fully absolving the forever empty vessel that was Eldon's conscious, preparing him for a new week of redemption.

For his neighbor Jim, it was brutally beating his children for the smallest infraction, for his friend Carl; well good old Carl raped his own daughters. Like mindless robots these men would calmly stroll into church with their wives and victims in tow, all would be forgiven or ignored. Jesus was a comforting friend to these sinners. Their crimes would go unpunished, their souls cleansed just for the asking.

As the organ would warm up and the change would start to clank in the offering plate, the clapping and hollering would begin. Their souls were now renewed and their hearts content.

Some would be overcome with the "spirit" and dance around in circles with their eyes rolled back in their heads waving their arms in the air and rapidly clapping their hands, as they were again set free. They could now resume destroying the lives of the innocent, because the promise of redemption was as sure as the next sunrise. Forgiveness was never required from your victims, only from Jesus. How wonderful it was to be completely forgiven from all of your horrible acts by an unseen entity that has never suffered the brutalities of your hands or the sickness of your mind.

When Diana began to show, she was accused of fornicating with a boy down the street and thrown out. She ended up at a small church outside of Hillsboro, Ohio, where she gave stillbirth to a boy child in the basement of the church. She looked closely at this silent little boy that had come from her body, he was beautiful and perfect. She asked the Pastor why this baby was dead.

The Pastor of the church was an unusual man, who continually quoted bits and pieces of scripture.

His rhetoric was always carefully crafted to fit whatever situation he was trying to manipulate, always repeating "Father God, Lord Jesus," in a continual mindless stutter that seemed to synchronize with the change pouring into the Wednesday night and Sunday morning offering plates.

Pastor Williams was an unlicensed physician and faith healer or as a silent few in the community called him: "a god dammed lunatic."

The Lord hath taken your first-born Diana to be with and near him as punishment for your sins against God. The pastor then clutched Diana's nearly limp body as he slowly guided her barely conscious face to his. Praise God with me Diana, blessed are we before the Lord!

Diana cried and begged the pastor to pray with her, she begged God silently for death.

Diana ended up in a group foster home with a local family. She was blessed with nearly three years of clean clothes and regular meals. It was the calm before the storm.

Just before her sixteenth birthday, Diana met twenty-five-year-old Leon Robarts, who on his very best day was never sober past breakfast and never without complete disregard for whatever woman he was presently violating.

Decisions in life were always real easy for Leon, and no one-word could be used to define him. His greatest burdens in life were unzipping his drawers or reaching for the opener that he kept on a chain fixed to his belt loop so he could crack a beer.

The only time Leon approached sobriety was the few hours a day that he would sleep. He lived in a 1939 Prairie Schooner travel trailer parked in his uncle's field. His Uncle Birch had swindled the trailer from someone.

The trailer home was a rotted up, leaky roofed, stinking hell pit. Other than for right up next to the wall board, the stained nap of the carpet is all that remained on the floor. Diana became immediately pregnant and for almost nine months now, she had tried to make it a home.

The moldy smelling trailer home was only interrupted by the stink of Leon. Earlier that day it had all began.

Where's my God dammed breakfast Diana?

Leon, there ain't no food in this trailer. I'm sick on the commode darlin, please bring me a smoke and set with me for a minute, I got the morning sickness bad.

Just glaring at Diana with glossy half-opened eyes and a perpetual hangover, Leon backhanded her in the face… puke'in….. bitch.. I spect whenever you hear my car comin up the lane tonight you'll get in a better way right quick. . . I know you hear me cow.

This wasn't the first time Diana had been hit by Leon, or the second. She never fought back or even raised her voice at him. Diana always viewed the abuses she suffered as some on the spot personal inadequacy. It wasn't punishment; instead, it was something never defined, something that just happened, an accepted act of violence that occurred whenever she was unable to anticipate something that she certainly should have.

The door slammed and Leon left. Nearly bursting with child, she slowly raised herself up from the floor and indirectly looked at herself in the mirror.

She could never look at herself in any mirror straight on, that would force a glimpse she could not face; it was always at an angle insuring that she would never look herself directly in the eye. Her cheek was split open and she watched as the blood dripped into the little round rusty trailer sink with a rhythm that sounded like the second hand of a clock ticking as the drops landed, each spreading out forming intricate patterns on the rust stained porcelain.

Diana prayed for Jesus to forgive Leon. She wanted this baby so bad, she wanted a family that she could create, where people loved each other and celebrated holidays together. She dreamed of receiving flowers and a box of candy when the baby came.

Everywhere in the dull paneled and poorly lit trailer home Diana had found haunting faces within the patterns of the wood paneling; she named them, she knew them. She had also tacked up dozens upon dozens of magazine ad pictures on any wall that would hold them.

There were couples holding hands swinging back and forth as they walked up freshly poured concrete sidewalks to their newly purchased brick homes.

These people wore modern clothes while setting in shiny new cars with gapped toothed smiling kids poking out each of the windows. They leaned on beached boats with coolers on their shoulders for an afternoon of picnicking on a beautiful beach at a pristine lake. A lake surrounded by groves of towering pine trees, craftsman styled cabins with porch swings and pots of coffee setting at the edge of large rock fireplaces.

Diana acted as if these ads were her family portraits, all of these nearly perfect families setting around perfect tables with plenty of food served at proper place settings, everyone grateful smiling and happy.

These healthy looking and good-smelling people from Rockwell wore plaid dresses and freshly starched white shirts with perfect teeth and perfect hair. They graced the walls of a decrepit old trailer they would never see or could never imagine seeing.

These people were Diana's family, and she had conversations with them, saying "please," "thank you" and "would you like some coffee," desperately hoping that some small portion of these pictures would become something she could one day touch and smell.

Diana would immerse herself in this beautiful world. She would travel to coastal Maine and the Rocky Mountain forest, always dreading the rapid trip home, reached simply by opening her weary eyes.

She carried her favorite magazine ad with her everywhere; it was a 1940 Swift Meat advertisement of a family setting around a table in front of a fireplace, all heads bowed. This family was her family, she knew them all by name and she loved them dearly. When things were unbearable Diana would carefully unfold this ad and pray that she was praying at the table with this family, this was Diana's existence, this was her world.

She craved the smell of fresh laundry and a pot of coffee, to her this meant peace, it meant that things were right. This imaginary world was the only love Diana ever understood and to her it was just as real as the hatred she had known all of her life.

Diana wrote her thoughts down; she wrote the most beautiful things. She described a world which she did not physically occupy, but it was where she resided.

 She wrote a poem for the child she carried:

My dear baby, my darlin-to-be, Mommy loves you so much even before your eyes see. When you are in my arms and you come to know me, I shall guide you through this world so wonderfully.

She would read this over and over to her unborn child and clutch it together with her favorite magazine ads as she would pray for the wonderful life that she dreamed of.

Chapter 2, Life at the Station

Leon spent his days at a service station owned by his Uncle Birch. It was the only grease pit in town. Birch had quite the racket at the station convincing people whenever possible that major repairs were needed. Major repairs typically meant swapping parts or just stealing whatever they wanted from the cars they would supposedly service.

Out-o'towners were easy prey and a peak through the tall plank fence in the back revealing two acres full of cars and parts stood testament to their success. You dare not ask for the oil to be checked, Birch and Leon were both masters at rigging the engine so that it would start acting up a mile down the road.

With a quick tow back to the garage your car or your wallet would be held forever prisoner.

You would either pay the bill or have a mechanics lien levied against you within a few hours. Quite the racket these boys had.

You bastard sons o bitches, I will be back, I WILL be back God dammit! I will be back with a lawyer . . .

To which Birch would reply . . . that'll be fine, but fer the time a bein get this heap of shit off my property before I start chargin ya for parkin. At this, he would push a car right out in the road if his former customer didn't first.

Their motto was - If it ain't broke, we'll dammed sure fix it till it is. There was always a fresh supply of Northern Kentucky and Southern Ohio hillbillies and the occasional Mountaineer. One crooked as a rusty nail neurotic sheriff served as judge whenever the threat of legal action arose.

There was one thing however that was consistently available at the station without fail, and that was a bottle of ice cold beer.

The county was bone dry, but for thirsty locals with 20 cents, a cold bottle of beer was always available at the station, day or night.

Ten cents of every beer sold went to the Sheriff who supplied the station with the beer that was hauled in his cruiser's trunk and back seat every other day or so from McGaw, Ohio right next to the Ohio River.

Twenty cents was almost double the wartime ceiling price for a bottle of beer, but if you're in a dry county and already breaking the law just buying the beer, there was certainly no reason to report anything. For a nickel less than one bottle of beer, you could have bought a gallon of gas, but gas didn't make you feel good and it was in limited supply wherever you could buy it. Birch Robarts had as much beer as you could ever want, and you never needed any ration stamps or books, just cash. Any other beer, legal or otherwise was at least two counties and a few gallons of fuel away. Business for Birch was good, real dammed good.

Long before there was such a thing as a drive through, Birch Robarts possibly had the very first. A fill up (in a bag) was six beers, and half a tank (in a bag) was three beers. A quart of "oil" (in a bag) was a single bottle.

Recently, they also started selling counterfeit cigarettes at almost half the retail price.

If Birch would have sold as much gasoline as beer and smokes, Shell Oil could have opened a refinery right next door. The beer was kept in a large cooler room that Birch had built himself. The ice man came twice during the week and made a special trip on Saturdays to bring a load of cedar sawdust to keep the ice covered.

Maybe it was the smell of the wet cedar sawdust you had to wipe off the bottle, but there was just something that made the beer from the station taste better than legally purchased suds. If there had to be a magic ingredient, it must have been the sheer convenience or the mystery of it getting from where ever it came from, then to the station and then into your hand - ice cold - right at the start of World War II.

Birch was rich by Waverly standards and so was the Sheriff, but it didn't show.

The Sheriff hated Leon Robarts with a passion, and so did almost everyone else. To the Sheriff, a dead Leon was preferred to a live one.

Leon had once been interrupted trying to convince the Sheriffs thirteen-year-old daughter Jenny to do some personal modeling for him.

Birch had reminded the Sheriff of their unique arrangement and the Sheriff was reluctantly convinced not to pursue the matter further.

Still, he hated Leon and watched his every move. The only thing Leon loved was the bottle and his dick whenever he was sober enough to put the later into action.

Gotta Get to Hillsboro

Diana got through the day smoking Old Golds, drinking Pepsi Cola and eating the broken bits of saltine crackers she had stuffed in her pockets from the last time she had a restaurant meal in town.

It was just about dark when she could hear Leon coming up the lane and she dreaded what was to come.

Leon stumbled through the door in his usual drunken fashion, tossing a large bag of fried chicken from the diner up on the table. Parts of the bag had turned translucent from the hot grease soaking through. The moldy smell of the trailer combined with cigarettes was temporarily replaced with the delicious combination of rosemary, thyme and pepper awash in hot lard.

Leon watched Diana with a drunken smirk, anticipating her day long appetite. After setting there for a good while, he began…

Hungry?

Yes, baby I am, so hungry.

Smells purdy dammed good don't it?

It does, darlin, real good, that seasonin makes my mouth water. I ain't had much today, actually I ain't had nuthin.

Well….you can jist keep ya dammed fingers off.

Come on baby, just one piece, just a thigh or drum? I'm eatin for two now?

After a long pause Leon slurs, you know how I hate yer beggin Diana.

Then don't make me beg, I'm starvin.

If there's any left, we can see if yer still hungry. Fat cow, if you would cook, you could eat.

Truth is there was never anything to cook. Truth is Diana had no idea how to cook and any pots or pans that did exist were in use catching the old and newly discovered drips from the ceiling anytime it rained.

Please darlin, please with sugar and honey. . . . . . I am so hungry…

At this, Leon went into his typical alcoholic rage, knocking Diana down the hallway, stepping on her hands each time she would try to get up, smacking her hard anytime she would make it to her knees.

As he beat her, Leon would giggle in a weird way, as if he were sort of embarrassed when he would hit her, but it was oddly pleasurable for him watching this pitiful pregnant woman roll around and beg. She was so vulnerable, and more than anything else, this truly delighted him.

Diana screamed and begged him to stop, but like every other time before he did not.

Leon…. darlin, please I'm carryin our baby. . . please.

You ain't carryin nuthin belongs to me.

Diana regained her senses in a pool of blood and amniotic fluid, her water had broken.

Leon was just setting there listening to the radio, humming along in his usual ignorant stupor, screaming at the radio if the signal would fade.

Without saying a word, Diana drug herself to an old Dodge with four bald tires, all nearly flat. She had carefully parked the old car on top of a small hill in the lane.

For many weeks she had been siphoning gas from Leon's car and Birch's Link Belt so she could make it to town when her baby came. Morning sickness and a mouth full of gasoline were as close as Diana would get to a breakfast most days.

She had one shot to coast start the car, knowing that she didn't have the strength to push the car back to the top of the hill if it didn't start. She thrashed herself to the car, pushing as she fell in to get it rolling down the hill. After slamming it into gear and several backfires, the old car chugged to life.

With every beat of her heart, Diana lost more blood; for almost an hour she drifted in and out of consciousness all the way to Hillsboro. She knew the preacher would deliver her baby, he would help her.

Diana realized that she was not in good shape. She had never allowed herself to remember the bad parts of her life but as she drove, her entire miserable life flashed before her eyes. Every rape, every brutal attack, every Christmas spent someplace different.

She unfolded her 1940 Swift ad and prayed with her family. She wasn't going to allow this life, her life, for her baby.

Diana wasn't really certain of her own birthday, she never had a birthday party or even received a present her entire life. She would love her baby and make sure that birthdays, holidays and everyday were filled with the joy she had never realized. She even forgave Leon; she thought that once he saw the baby everything would be okay, and that he would come to love her and their child.

Diana fell through the door of the parsonage. The pastor's oldest son Paul screamed for his father and they carried her into the basement. Diana went limp, Pastor Williams knew that Diana was dying and that there was no hope for her or the child. He could see the thrashing of an infant in her abdomen.

Paul ran to get the granny woman from down the street. Together they sliced open a near lifeless Diana, only to discover that there were two babies in her womb. Both of the babies had suffered severely. Both had been "beaten" before opening their eyes in this world. Both were barely alive.

The scene was utter carnage.

While the pastor had briefly attended medical school, he had not graduated and was not a licensed physician, certainly not a surgeon.

The Pike County Sheriff was called to make a report. The bits of wood splinters from the trailer home floor and paneling under her fingernails were certain proof that Diana had struggled and obviously had the hell beat from her.

The Sheriff knew that it was Leon and he hated himself for not immediately acting. However, he hated the thought of losing the extra money from the illegal beer sales just a little more than he hated the killer of the poor dead girl laying sliced open in front of him. He figured that Birch would expose the whole operation and that he would lose his elected post, family, and his complete way of life.

Still the Sheriff knew he had to say something, something must be done. So after discussing it with Birch, the next evening he had arranged for all of them to meet at the station.

As Birch and the Sheriff waited on Leon to show up, the Sheriff notices Birch rubbing his arm.

What's wrong with ya' arm Birch?

Don't know, damn near killin me up at the shoulder, it's a keepin me up at night.

Well, go have Doc take a peek at it.

Piss on that, gonna have to get to the point I cain't stand it a'fore I'd give that bastard a red cent.

Well, maybe not for you, but keepin me up at night is well past gettin to the point I can't stand it. You got any aspirins?

Yep, how many ya need?

Not fer me, fer ya' arm!

Can't take em, gimme nose bleeds.

Birch, five will get ya ten the bastard won't show.

I ain't a bettin, but he dammed sure better, he's livin on my dime, always has.

Birch, not to pry into yer private matters, but why do you put up with Leon? You've got to know the sumbitch is nuts.

Well Charlie, I do, I do. But you got to understand that Leon is all I have, and I dammed sure know I am all he has. I know that the righteous folks think that everything happens to you once the all mighty drops ya off here, well I don't believe that a'tall. Leon didn't have much of chance.

Not to bring too fine a point to it, but his mother, my sister Elizabeth was never right, NEVER. Leon shouldn't even be alive, how the bastard is stumps me.

So, do you know anything bout where this girl Diana came from Birch, or what her exact family name was?

Nope, can't say that I do, cause I don't. Don''t know a dammed thing bout her.

Well, neither does anyone else. Seems that she just blew in with the wind. She was a mess like I ain't never seen. It's sad, I'll tell ya that.

It is . . . dammed sad. I do believe her family name was Smith, but I wouldn't bet on it. I've only seen her one time, she was a sight. Kind of takes me back to my sister. But life goes on don't it?

Fer some it does, fer her it sure ain't.

A few minutes pass and Leon finally shows up, freshly bathed and without his usual accompanying body odor mixed with alcohol and cigarettes.

The Sheriff confronts Leon about Diana's death and the birth of the twins.

So . . . , what have you got to say about all this Leon?

Bout what?

About Diana.

I ain't sure what yer talkin bout?

QUIT playin games with me moron, you dammed sure know what I'ma talkin bout!

Well shit Sheriff . . . hell… I wouldn't have taken that whore into the sheets with your dick.

No, ya sure wouldn't have, but you'd take any old goat with yer own.

Hell, I just let her stay out at the trailer, those little bastard babies aren't mine, well shit . . .Sheriff. . . the whore came to me with child . . . I just . . . just uh . . .

You just what Leon, you JUST beat the livin hell out of her?

Never laid a hand on her, swear to the all mighty.

Bullshit. You were a gettin on with her, and yer the reason she was with child and yer the reason she's dead. And just to be sure, the *all mighty* has never listened to a word from yer sorry ass, swearin or otherwise.

Leon is looking down and the Sheriff is looking at him dead on. Birch is alternating between the two.

The Sheriff continues; Leon . . . I seen a bloody God dammed mess yesterday, a mess so terrible that I won't be forgetin it in this life.

A mess so gruesome and sad that I would surely like to clamp you by the neck and stick your bastard nose in it if I thought it would matter. I seen a young woman who had the hell beat out of her so bad she couldn't possibly give birth in the normal way. Fact is she was either dead or so close to bein dead they had to cut her wide open just to get the two babies out of her and they were barely holdin to life. Both of um had a full head of hair blacker than coal-eez ass, just like their daddy, right here, right now.

So, I ain't buy'in yer shit Leon, not a word of it, not a God dammed soul would. Poor girl had a magazine ad and a poem all folded up and clamped tight in her hand, don't know what that was about.

Just silence followed for a few seconds as Leon just sat there, staring off, not saying a word.

The Sheriff continues: Everybody in the county knows that pitiful thing was living at yer trailer, and everyone knows you treated her worse than a dammed dog. So cut the shit right now and tell the truth for the first time in yer life.

Leon was not a convincing liar.

Not acknowledging a single word of what the Sheriff had just said, Leon in a real nervous voice says; besides Sheriff, I'm a savin' myself . . . . . . for a lovely lady . . . . . . that daughter of yours . . . pretty young Jenny.

With a whoosh and a click, the Sheriff quickly drew and cocked his Colt, jamming it in Leon's throat under his chin, he grabbed Leon by the collar and lifted him off the floor.

You're a god damned idiot Leon, a worthless murderin' liar! You won't even breath the same air as my Jenny . . . you ignorant sumbitch, you ain't worth the hot lead I'm gonna put through your skull.

Birch interrupted the screaming by taking a three pound ball peen hammer to a thick steel plate on his work bench so hard that all ears were ringing.

Birch's screams seemed muted and all were nearly deaf.

Just a God dammed minute here, just one GOD dammed minute here, now Sheriff, we have a business to run here Goddamit, ALL of us are in business here and we can't let the passin' of some no account interfere with our affairs. Now dammit Charlie that's the way it's got to be.

The Sheriff lowered a sickeningly smirking Leon to the floor, popped the clip and discharged the chambered bullet intended for Leon, catching it with his other hand all in one smooth motion. He walked toward the door, walking back and forth wringing his hands and squeezing his head.

Now give a hello to that pretty wife and your sweet girl Jenny for me, Leon mumbled.

The Sheriff instantly turned and while clenching both fists and pointing at Leon while screaming;

You even look at my girl again, and you're a dead man.

Birch smacked Leon on the back of the head and with a slobbering clinched mouth told him to shut his big yap. Birch then loudly piped in, he's an idiot Sheriff just a damned idiot, he's just play'n Sheriff.

It didn't matter; the Sheriff hated the worthless piece of shit that was Leon Robarts.

The Sheriff left.

Birch was madder than hell. For the first time in a long time he told Leon how much.

Leon fer the second or maybe third time in yer wretched life, I saved yer sorry ass.

I am the only reason yer still breathin, do you preciate that you dumb sumbitch?

I coulda handled him.

Him who?

The Sheriff.

Bullssssshit, with his 1911a in your throat, hammer fully back, you wern't handlin nuthin, not even the shit collectin in yer drawers. You was a second or two away from where you rightly oughta be. Yer jist a God dammed waste Leon and from this day on, I'll not step in.

Unknown to most, the Sheriffs wife had many affairs with men in the area. Her current liaison just happened to be Leon Robarts. The Sheriff was oblivious to this and had no idea that the person he hated the most was his wife's current lover.

Every time the Sheriff would make his pilgrimage down to the Ohio River for beer, Leon would make his pilgrimage to the Sheriff's house to tend to the immediate needs of his wife.

She would be fully nude and wait on Leon to scuttle on over and give the old shave and a haircut at the back door. At two bits he would slowly crack open the door.

In her sweetest voice, Janet would coax Leon on in . . .

You got sumthin for Mommy today Leon?

Yes I do madam Sheriff, why yes I do. I got a whole bunch a sumthin fer ya.

Well come on in and let's see.

This had been going on for several years. This woman who seemed so normal on the outside would instruct Leon to do things that the Sheriff could not even imagine. Leon took great pride in this, in his mind it seemed to even things out a little bit.

A drunken Leon would stumble in, drop his drawers and put the Sheriff's old police hat on and say, Mam, I believe yer under arrest.

Chapter 3, A Burial and the Babies

Diana was buried in a furniture crate hastily painted with a cross by the pastor's son. He picked some corn flowers and tied them into a bunch, placing them on her coffin. They were the only flowers she ever received.

No headstone, no relatives, no tears, no prayers, not a God dammed soul, just the pastor's wife trying to get pastor Williams to hurry up so that she would not be late for her knitting group.

The only thing that accompanied Diana to the grave was blame for everything that had happened in her short life.

As the forgiven must, blame the desperate for being so, blame the ignorant for being so, blame the unholy for being so, blame the dead who needed help so badly in this life. Throw stones still at the spirit, for the body will be taken by this earth, *where many shall soon be.*

The county did insist however that the church carry out a search for any earthly relatives the boys may have. No one stepped forward.

With the unmistakable clunk and echo of a large mechanical embosser, and just daylight shining through an old county office, the brother's birth certificates were stamped by the clerk after being typed by his assistant.

They read as follows:

Name(s) BASTARD 1 and BASTARD 2,

Father: Unknown,

Status: Unknown,

Age: Unknown,

Address: Unknown,

Race: Unknown.

Mother: Diana Smith(family name unsure),

Status: Transient-deceased,

Age: 16 years – aprox.,

Address: Unknown,

Race: Caucasian

Several months passed and the church had elected to raise the boys under the care of Pastor Williams and his family, he had named them Hugh and Ursal.

It was becoming obvious that the boys were not fully normal. Their appearance was odd and they seldom made a noise.

They would open their small mouths but sounds would rarely come out. They would follow you around the room with their young eyes.

It seemed that any time you were looking at them, they were looking back. Their eyes were so dark that you could not distinguish a pupil.

The boys were unusual and Pastor Williams's wife insisted they were evil and the product of an unclean and sinful union. Soon she would not care for them in any capacity. Instead, pastor Williams forced his fourteen-year-old son Paul to help him administer all of the care for the boys.

The local boys made fun of the preacher's son; they said he was a "wet nurse to the longheaded retards." He knew their little songs all too well.

"Little brother's retards, little brother's retards give your titties to the retards.

Oh look boys, he has one titty full of retard milk for each of he's little retard brothers.

Go nurse your little retards, we hear um crying for you mommy."

Every time he went out of the house, someone was singing a new song or saying the worst things imaginable.

His anger turned into contained rage, young Paul Williams had a storm brewing in him. He officially hated his life, his father and all of those around him. He cried when no one looked, frustration could not begin to describe his pain.

Chapter 4, Birch and Leona Robarts

Birch Robarts was the poorest *looking* man you could ever lay eyes on. Looks sure can be deceiving, and in Birch's case they certainly were. His never washed, once denim overalls were shiny with years of imbedded grease and grime.

When he smiled the rotten center of every tooth was visible. He always had a half chewed cigar in his mouth, never lit, but always dripping wet.

Birch lived amongst decades of accumulated papers, grocery sacks, and calendars that made up his small living area at the station.

There were car parts still in boxes from the 1920s, huge stacks of automotive manuals, and box after box of petrified and never opened Christmas candy.

A thick layer of dust combined with grease covered almost everything. Large ropes of dust and grime hung from the ceiling in every corner.

The house smelled like you just removed the gas cap from a lawnmower that had been setting for a decade, like old varnished gasoline mixed with vulcanized tires, tobacco spit and grease from the kitchen.

There were no doors between the rooms instead just "stiff as a board" grease soaked curtains with a very faded pattern that could no longer be identified becoming visible towards the top. Each hanging from a drooping spring loaded rod in the top of the doorway.

Birch had one skillet, one fork, one spoon etc. More than one of anything meant that it would be dirty of just setting. Everything he ate came from the same cast iron skillet that doubled as a plate.

Birch lived on a breakfast of three eggs over easy cooked in browned butter, a lunch of coffee and a super that consisted of one half-pound of fried loose hamburg with salt and pepper cooked in browned butter with half a loaf or so of white bread to sop up the skillet. Each day and every day, this was what sustained Birch Robarts.

He had no radio, subscribed to no publications, and only received information from the locals. Of the thousands upon thousands of bottles of beer that he had illegally sold through the years, he never drank one.

Birch was like a grimy time capsule, nothing had ever really changed except his age. He did not celebrate any holidays and had not traveled more than one hundred miles from his birthplace in his entire life. What he didn't know, he didn't want to know. What he didn't have, he didn't need to have and that's how he lived.

A photograph that few had ever seen was still hanging in a side room, it was a framed picture of a smartly dressed young man and his beautiful wife. The young man was Birch with his wife Leona who had left him many years prior.

Continual disappointment had become an accepted way of life for Birch; in his younger years it hurt, now it was just a matter of getting through the day and on to the next.

Birch purchased the station along with the three acres of ground that was a wrecking yard and the fifty-acre field that Leon now lived on for only $200.

The seller of the properties had made an error and omitted a zero at the end of the listed price.

Birch began his swindling early on by threatening legal action if the seller did not honor the amount listed on the signed contract.

His business started out slowly and money was real tight, in fact they were barely making it. He started out as a pump and wash man learning the mechanical end of things as he went.

Because business at the station was struggling, Leona took work as a part-time waitress at a speakeasy described as a restaurant during the day and a telephone operator from 7 p.m. to 12 a.m. four days a week. She lived in Cincinnati during the week, only coming home on the weekends. She shared a small third floor apartment with another young lady during the week, her name was Betty Bailey.

Leona and Betty were fast friends and they lived it up. They honked in every tonky and tonkyed in every honk. They were chain smoking Flappers, hemlines all the way up the goody trail with morals barely a degree north of their male (sometimes female) pursuers.

They were hip before it became hip to be. Flatwheeler's be dammed, these girls were moving up by any and all means.

They only wore undergarments for the week or so a month they <u>had</u> to stay home. The lucky young men who coaxed these ladies to set on their laps would get quite the unexpected surprise. The girls called it: "leaving a little kiss to remember me by."

Cincinnati was loaded with fine clothing shops, nice places to eat, and lots of men pretending to have lots of money. It was in fact one fine place to be for a pretty country girl with strawberry blonde hair, a curvy figure and an empty purse.

The clean shaven city boys smelled good all of the time. They weren't shy with pleasing comments either. Coming home to Waverly was getting harder each time knowing that the only thing waiting for you was a perverted little nephew and a greasy husband with tobacco juice running down a weeks' worth of stubble, barely a nickel in his pocket.

A few months after taking work in Cincinnati, Leona was barely coming home at all.

A few weeks after that, she officially began accepting the advances of a fairly successful man with whom she became acquainted. She promptly divorced the heartbroken Birch and quickly married the Mr. Bank Account she had so immediately fallen in love with.

Before the rushed wedding Betty made fun of Leona, fully realizing her "condition."

So you dropped the *jake* only for a new *handcuff* huh?

I'm in love.

Nah . . .you're in trouble doll baby, I've seen you in action . . . you enjoy the ride to much for anything like love to be involved.

Well, I care for him deeply.

Nah, I ain't buyin it dear. Ya "cared" for the *jake* a little to "deeply" and now ya gotta snag a wallet or move back to sticks with *jake* before the bread rises and those perfect tits of yours turn to droopy old mumsy spigots.

Well, thanks for them particulars Betty darlin', I'm sick enough without em' yah know?

There is another option dear, If you wanna get back to business, I know a man who can make it all go away.

Yeah, and maybe me too . . .No, no . . . . . . NO.

Fine then deary, convince the new *handcuff* that the little bun is his, or it's plaid aprons and second hand picnic dresses for you, the *jake* and the lil' pre-vert.

Betty's assessment was every bit as brutal as the situation. What young and beautiful Leona Robarts would keep a secret for nearly 23 years was that she was five weeks along carrying Birch's child when she left, and eight weeks along when she married Mr. Frederick Lestor.

Birch had begged her out of some departing pleasures and this had left her in the market for a mighty quick marriage.

Birch's life effectively stopped when his wife left him. His time with Leona would be the only time Birch would have a relationship with any woman for the rest of his life.

Ironically he fell in love with his former wife's only true love, money. Just like his former wife, Birch was so in love with money that ultimately, it was the only thing that mattered.

The difference was that for Birch spending it was never an option, for his ex-wife it was in fact the only option.

At exactly the same time that Birch would be stuffing rolls of cash into mason jars and covering them in cedar dust, Leona would be unloading hundreds from the once deep - but ever rising - pockets of the new man at the finest shops in Cincinnati.

Birch's scratch was compliments of his thievery and a county full of alcoholics.

Leona's cash was all from the new man who craved that sweet country pussy from Pike County so much that he was already going crazy and broke just trying to keep it all for himself.

How it all Began

Leon Robarts never knew who his father was, neither did his mother Elizabeth, she was just grateful that her prayers were answered and that Leon appeared to be fully Caucasian.

Elizabeth was Birch's older sister, and her life was a tragic one. In 1920, Elizabeth died when Leon was three years old. Upon learning of Elizabeth's death, Birch had lamented over little Leon for several weeks. Finally his conscious got the better of him and he climbed in his truck and headed toward Washington Court House, Ohio to retrieve Leon from what the locals called the orphans' farm. It was kind of a boys' only orphanage on a working farm. It was run by the Schneidling family up in Fayette County.

Leon hopped up in his Uncle Birch's truck and scooted right over next to him. Birch talked with Leon the best he could.

Now…ya know that yer mammy is dead, right boy?

Yep, Leon shook his head yes.

Birch was teary eyed, but Leon couldn't see him. So, yer mom was my sister and now yer gonna live with me, oka dokie?

Yep.

Can you talk boy? Can you say sumthin other'n yep?

Yep, Leon just laughed without smiling.

We're gonna stop at the Roebucks an git ya some clothes and boots, that alright boy?

Leon laid his head on Birch falling asleep leaning on Birch's side. Birch laid his arm on Leon between the gears. He knows the hell that had been Leon's life, but Leon will never know the hell that Birch and his sister Elizabeth had grown up in.

Driving back to Waverly, Birch looked down at little Leon sleeping on his leg and he thought about his own childhood along with his sister in the early 1900s.

They were raised at the edge of Newport, Kentucky in the poorest part of town. Regular meals with the trimmings were rare. They usually ate twice a day. A cheap cut of fatty meat and a turnip, no salt, no pepper, maybe a wild onion, but that's it.

Birch remembers hearing Andus the old bone and rag man coming down their street singing his song:

"Any old rags or bones today. . . . . . . , cause I wants em fore you throws em away . . . . I takes em now or I takes em later, cause I'ma beggin . . . fo yous I sho cater."

Andus would loudly sing his song, occasionally varying the lyrics. He would slowly make his way down the street, barely moving along. He drove a team of huge old draft mules that pulled a giant wagon heaped on one side with rags of every type and bones on the other side.

The man picked up rags and bones to be re-used and made into paper, combs, gelatin and various other things.

Birch and Elizabeth would run down and hop up on the wagon riding it for a few blocks talking with Andus. His mules were named Sawney and Speckin.

Between his begging songs Andus would act out the mules' voices, acting as if the mules were talking to each other, one bitchin about the other for not pulling hard enough or anything you could imagine two huge draft mules side by side saying to each other.

"Lordy Speckin, yous get in'na unyon grass? . . . Oh no Sawney I eats cleaned oats and fresh dropped apples, yous surely wiffin yous own knotty tail!"

They would all laugh so hard. It was one of Birch's fondest memories from childhood.

Birch remembers how poor they were and how hard life was, how fast he had to grow up. He knew that his sister Elizabeth had been abused all of her life. Neither of them ever remembered their real father or a single word of discussion about him.

Their stepfather, Ross Setzer was originally from Arkansas. He had beaten both of them repeatedly, once just for eating a piece of fruit without asking. Ross argued with Birch and Elizabeth's mother almost every day, sometimes violently. Daring anyone to say a word in protest, Ross would smack their mother so hard that she would fall to the floor weeping.

She would quickly arise while falsely smiling at her children as if nothing had happened. Despite her forced smile, the vacant look of desperation in her eyes always told the real story.

Life was dammed hard, and no one beyond ear shot gave a shit who lived and who died.

Ross Setzer was just one of those men who seemed to operate with complete immunity in all situations. He was always half smiling, friendly and almost charming to those who didn't know him, a brutally abusive bastard to those who did.

Their long, dark shotgun apartment was a depressing place to live. Only the front room and the bedroom at the rear had any windows.

Ross had insisted that Birch and Elizabeth call him "Daddy Ross." It made Birch sick and he hated to say it. He had been thumped in the back of the head many times for not saying it.

Elizabeth was kind of a stocky girl, well developed by the age of thirteen. Birch never liked how *Daddy Ross* looked at his sister, always sweet talking her, wanting her to set on his lap.

By the time Elizabeth was fifteen years old, her stepdad Ross started fooling around with her every day, just as soon as her mother walked out the door for work. This had been going on for almost a month. Birch would be shooed off, while Elizabeth would be forced to stay inside.

One afternoon when Birch had come home from the ball field early, *Daddy Ross* had Elizabeth behind locked door. She was sobbing, and begging him to leave her alone.

Birch listened to the muffled conversation on the other side of the door a few steps down the hall. Welling up with tears, it was all he could do to keep from busting down the door. Somehow, he hung on and continued to listen with a knot so tight in his throat that he struggled for each breath.

He knew Ross was taking his trousers off because he could hear the whoosh of his belt and his pocket change clanging in the bowl on top of the dresser.

Ross was talking real low.

Now Liz . . . . . . , I've uh, taken up a special fondness fer ya, and when we gets the chance, you and I, uh well . . . we . . . we gonna be lovers like in'na picture shows cept different . . . . Fact is, we gonna jist love the hell from one anotha, jist as I says and whens I says, folla me?

Yes *Daddy Ross.*

If I take down my drawers, yer gonna beg for whatever I'ma offerin, ya folla me now?

Yes *Daddy Ross.*

Unless it's yer dirty time, if I says bend over, you get them knees on the hassock and stick that fat ass up. If ya give me any lip, any lip 'tall, I'ma gonna beat the shit right outta of ya and you'll do it anyhow just with bruises, if bruises is what ya need, folla me?

Yes *Daddy Ross.*

If'ins yer dirty time, you make a pony whip with that hair so's I know it. If'n I grab you by that pony whip, you gonna open that fat yap and take daddy Ross on in without gaggin or bitin or I'll beat the life from yer lumpy ass. Ya folla me?

Yes *Daddy Ross.*

Elizabeth was bawling with her eyes closed and she begged Ross for a sheet to cover herself.

Screaming at her to shut up, Ross smacked Elizabeth hard on the side of her head, knocking her into a dresser and then to the floor.

Now, you git up and dance fo me, raise them lumpy god dammed legs like a show girl, raise um up high, that's right, you a gettin it . . . . git ya hands off'n nim titties . . .

Elizabeth was sobbing and trying to dance completely nude for Ross as he sat there, smacking his hand on his leg while stomping out an acceptable tempo for her to dance to. Birch could hear the boards creaking and feel the thuds of Elizabeth's feet hitting the floor.

Finally Ross let her stop.

We ain't gonna converse bout this to no one else, folla me?

Yes *Daddy Ross*.

It's nobody else's concern.

Elizabeth just stood there fully nude and crying, completely out of breath, continuing to answer Ross in a machine like and detached fashion, like she was someone else.

Birch had stayed crouched down the hall, listening the entire time. The situation had left him so sick that he nearly fainted. He slipped out undetected and walked around watery eyed for many hours sort of drifting in and out of reality, actually forgetting where he was at. It was hard for his mind to get a grip on things, he couldn't imagine how Elizabeth was coping, for weeks she was barely talking to him and she would never look him in the eye. One thing was now certain, *Daddy Ross* Setzer had to pay.

After watching every step Ross would take on his walk home from work, and thinking it out for several days, Birch thought he was ready.

He waited for Ross to walk home from his second watch position as a security guard at the tannery plant he worked at. After waiting for nearly an hour, Birch jumped out in an overgrown narrow alley and surprised Ross about three blocks from home holding a three foot section of rusted iron pipe like a ball bat.

Well . . . well . . . looka here . . . a stumpy an a lumpy fat little Birch Robarts . . . well . . . *Ross was half chuckling. . .*

I sposed you was Liz in the corner of my eye. Boy, jist a smiggin more titty an you'd be a spittin image of that plumpy sister o'yers. You wantin ta dance for daddy Ross too?

Breathing hard and staggering back and forth in slow circles, Birch says nothing.

Whatcha got there boy, a pipe? . . . . huh . . . Whatcha ya eyes all watery fer boy? Ross was smiling at Birch with a big chew in his jaw.

I sposin you just jealous a ole *Daddy Ross*, pleasurin that fatty sister 'yers. I knowed you hear'in her beggin me, she won't leave daddy Ross be fer a minute. Why . . . ever'day she's a wrestlin my drawers off . . . jist soon as yer mammy's out ta door . . . Course, I knowed you probly a peekin in, a watchin ole daddy Ross . . . that right boy?

Ross was squinty eyed and smiling in the worst sort of way.

Birch takes a partial swing at Ross's head as he leans towards him.

You up ta bat boy? . . . . . . huh . . . . . . You   gonna hit   me? . . . . . . You gonna bring **HELL** on to *Daddy Ross*?

Birch just stood there breathing even harder with tears pouring down his cheeks, almost frozen stiff too afraid to say a word.

Y'aint a talkin huh? . . . . Well . . . I's set this here lunch bucket down and we do some talkin, rough talkin . . . . . . daddy Ross bout to teach you a hard, hard lesson . . . . . . gonna thump yer skull boy . . . Yer mammy won't be missin ya, alls ya do is pig up the grub . . . Tobacco juice was running down Ross's chin on both sides.

As Ross turned to set his lunch pail on the ground, with one hard blow from the side, Birch split Ross' head like a ripe pumpkin.

Birch stood over him watching him. As Ross tried to reach one quivering hand up, Birch stomped his hand as hard as he could, every dying finger crushed under his heel.

He threw the pipe in a thicket and took off.

Birch had killed *Daddy Ross* Setzer with a dirt filled pipe, he was barely fourteen years old and he would never tell a soul his entire life.

He cried lookin at Ross with his head split open just layin there with his body jerking and convulsing, but he also felt relieved because he hated the son of a bitch.

Knowing what Elizabeth had been through was much worse than looking at the bastard with his head crushed, dying right there in front of you.

Ross owed everybody and their brother money, the cops just figured that somebody had finally collected.

Unfortunately for Birch and especially Elizabeth, their Mother's next beau was even worse than *Daddy Ross* Setzer.

After being violated so many times, forced sex had become a normal way of life for Elizabeth and she no longer rejected it.

With the help of a granny woman, slippery elm bark had eliminated most of the mistakes and early still birth one or two more. This was more than Birch could bring himself to understand and he had moved out for good before his fifteenth birthday, never returning.

Like so many young women had before and would after her, Elizabeth mortally confused what she perceived as loving affection with a mindless dick's desire to ejaculate into the most vulnerable receptacle available. Brutal sex, even rape became love, at least the only love Elizabeth Robarts would ever know. Polite society could not have been further away.

Elizabeth's life plummeted out of control and got to the point that the smallest things were all that counted; a dry match, a cigarette, five minutes of hot water, electric service for a single day a month. Real things like love, a home, and a family were so far out of reach they were too painful to reckon and would never be considered.

Leon's little bed was a large Old Reliable Coffee crate that he had stuffed with a World War I surplus wool blanket for a mattress. He had two toys, a truck with no wheels and one old passenger car from a train set.

The only food he regularly received was from an elderly Negro woman who lived in the same tenement house. He lived on soda biscuits and salt pork gravy.

He would swipe a bottle or two of milk every few days from the better parts of town.

Dairy service wouldn't go down the street where he lived with his mother. Leon couldn't speak his own name, but he could run like a scared rabbit. He would swipe a quart of milk and knock it down in about a minute. He was also a dammed good aim with the empty or partial empty if anyone dared to pursue. He had plugged several people in the past trying to "reclaim" their dairy on the fly, nearly killed a few folks. A half full quart of milk flung straight up in the air at a full run delivers one dammed serious blow if you're in its return path.

Leon just wasn't normal and that's the only way to describe him. As a child he was so unbelievably cruel that he would climb a tree just to knock a bird's nest down so he could stomp on, or drown the babies one at a time in a puddle.

He would tie a string around their neck or foot and lower them again and again in the water until they thrashed their final time.

With bare feet and arms crossed, a little Leon would chase down and stomp on cockroach's so fast that it looked like some exotic Spanish dance. It was dammed near as amazing to watch as it was disgusting.

His little legs would be flying. He would stomp the roach's so hard that they would make a loud popping sound. They sounded like muted fire crackers going off. This was Leon's favorite thing to do. Everyone in the tenement house would utilize his services, if nothing else but for the entertainment.

It was suspected that Leon was abused by one or more of his mother's many late night guests. He was certainly abused by his mother.

Romping on some whore all night long, only to be awakened by a little boy making loud gear shifting sounds while *rolling* a truck with no wheels under the bed just scared the hell out of a lot of men.

Then to look down and see a little black haired crossed eyed boy with pissy pants looking up from the floor at you at 5 a.m. thoroughly enraged a few more. Elizabeth Robarts was always a fuck of last resort.

The first sentence a little Leon spoke was "git da hell outta here" he thought it was his name. It was a big joke at the station when Leon was a little boy everyone hollered "git da hell outta here," Leon would come running, everyone would laugh and Leon would just stare. "Little git da hell outta here" became his nickname.

The only thing that separated Elizabeth from actually being a whore was those who knew her. She had died of advanced venereal disease. Leon had lain in bed with his mother's corpse for almost three days before she was discovered. It had been the most peaceful time he ever had with his mother. As mean as she was to him, he clung to her body when they tried to remove her and it took three men to keep him away. The loud wailing screams that came from little Leon were so pitiful it was hard to believe they were human. It was an event no one involved with would ever want to recall.

Leon had never attended school a day in his life. Everything he knew was from watching and listening to others.

At ten years, Leon had the body and intentions of an eighteen-year-old man. After having the shit kicked out of him from the time he was crawling, he was tough, real tough.

While living with Birch, Leon raped a twenty four-year-old out-of-town woman when he was just twelve years old. She tried to press charges but there were not laws at the time to support such a thing.

As she refused to submit to a medical examination, no real proof that he had committed a crime could be provided.

By the time he was fourteen years old Leon could beat the shit right out of most grown men. Only a fool or a stranger would mix it up with Leon Robarts. He was brutal, he had nothing to lose, and he would kill a man with no remorse whatsoever.

In Leon's world there were no rules in life, accept those immediately imposed by the strong and immediately adhered to by the weak, and that's the way it was for him.

Leon could not separate sexual acts from violent acts, in his mind they went together like gin and quinine water.

He had hair so black that it always looked greasy and usually was. He wasn't a physically unattractive man and he could actually be quite charming. But to be sure, every emotion that Leon portrayed, every expression he could muster, everything that appeared remotely human was contrived with purpose.

Although he never smiled, Leon laughed at everything, everything was funny.

As a little boy he laughed to keep from crying, and at times he appeared to combine the two. As an adult, he laughed instead of crying, never combining the two. It was the only emotion he showed and even it was misplaced.

What Leon lacked in knowledge was partially replaced with his ability to read people, especially vulnerable women. However, to be certain, Leon was damaged, FUBAR, a God dammed waste of good air. He always had been and he always would be.

You don't wake up every morning watching your mother getting violently fucked by a different man and turn out to be normal.

A woman who never even hugs you, erotically giving herself completely to a stranger cannot be rectified by a young mind.

By the time Leon was three years old he had witnessed more sex than most people would have seen or experienced in their entire life.

Leon would accurately mimic his mother's sexual actions, and the sounds that she would make, sometimes while she was engaged in the act.

At times she would laugh and other times she would become enraged and kick him across the floor. More than anything else, this truly delighted her, watching little Leon tumble across the floor. Leon would just laugh and she would kick him harder. Kicks became hugs, the only hugs Leon would get.

Like many in this life, Leon desperately needed help from the time he was born, but it wasn't to be.

He would simply become another one to blame for societies moral failings because no one would reach out to a little boy who hadn't known a loving day in his life.

Instead, polite society would patiently wait for the illness and mistreatment of a tragic childhood to manifest itself into a life-long disaster.

Prosecution always takes the place of prevention. Even today, every law in the land makes it so. You've got to be responsible and take charge of yourself, even if you can't define who or what you are, even if you've grown up in filth and violence, never setting foot in a school, never having a proper meal setting at a table with others. So what we get is the brutal reality of atrocities never married up to a conscious, a conscious never married up to polite society, a conscious never knowing or feeling anything ever but what the eyes have seen and the ears have heard. When tragedy is all that's witnessed, tragedy is all that's retained, and it doesn't go away, it DOES NOT go away.

Instead, it's passed on. It repeats itself; it balls up and unwinds for generations, sometimes manifesting itself in ways that are unimaginable to the reasonably sane mind. Yet we always act as if we just can't believe it. In truth there isn't much of anything that we shouldn't believe.

Birch tolerated Leon, he fed Leon, gave him a dry bed and to a point he pitied Leon. Birch was always plagued with his own demons. Leona divorcing him had smacked his mind forever silly. He didn't know how to raise a kid and he didn't much give a shit.

Rollin up cash for a fresh Mason jar had become Birch's only concern.

Reaching adulthood, Leon's evolved therapy would be a daily intake of alcohol that would kill most and a life of violent acts against any woman or girl unlucky enough to cross his path.

For those who have evolved without right and wrong, they are words with no meaning or purpose. Right was whatever you could get by with and wrong was whatever somebody else forced on to you.

Little "Get the hell outta here" had become, "Hold real still fo me now . . . or I'll knock 'em purdy teeth down ya fuckin' throat."

The Sheriff

Sheriff Charles "Charlie" Gifford was a tall lanky guy, a strong wind would seem to knock him over. He was a total worry wart; they didn't come more neurotic.

This man worried about the color of pavement. He worried about life so much that he couldn't enjoy any part of it. Everything was for Jenny and his wife. That's why he did what he did, for them, only for them. He quietly talked to himself, kind of mumbling most all of the time.

The only thing Charlie Gifford actually enjoyed doing was fly-fishing, and he was masterful at it.

He studied nature and insects. He would create flies that under his control would exactly mimic the actions of the specific insects he had thoroughly studied.

He had set up a special aquarium tank in his garage with magnified glass on one side so he could watch how the insects would land on the water; how they would thrash on the surface and even sink.

He could have made a handsome living doing what he loved, but like many in this life, he never even considered it, it just never crossed his mind.

He stumbled onto the bootleg beer business by complete accident. One afternoon he had pulled off to help a man with a flat tire only to find out that the man had a trunk full of beer and cigarettes.

The Sheriff was curious about this and made inquiry:

Friend, that's a load of Beer and cigarettes you got there, serve half this state for week or so . . .

Just headed home "friend." No law against a man enjoying some suds at the domicile is there?

I suppose not.

Without any reason to suspect anything else, the Sheriff sent him on his way.

However later that afternoon the Sheriff witnessed Birch Robarts rapidly swinging a door open at his garage, hurrying the man and his car in as if he knew him.

The Sheriff had known Birch for years. He went to see him later that evening. When he arrived Birch almost appeared to be waiting for him.

He slowly walked up to greet him.

How r ya Birch?

Fair to midland, I'd say. And yerself?

Well, I'm on the slant Birch, scratchin towards the peak, always a slidin back to the valley.

You ain't alone brother, you ain't alone.

Birch, I pulled a man over today and helped him with he's spare.

Um huh.

Then uh . . . later I saw him here in town.

Uh huh.

It seems yer on real friendly terms with this fella, invited him in real dammed quick, car AND all . . .

Uh huh.

Well, either he was headed to a large picnic or perhaps there is some other explanation fer he's payload.

I ain't gonna lie, been gone on fer several years now Charlie.

That so?

Yep, that's so. People gonna buy it someplace, why not here?

Well, prohibition never ended in Pike County, that's why not here.

C'mon Charlie, well if you blow this up now, why yer gonna look like a dammed fool. Every one of my drive up regulars votes fer ya. They ain't gonna be real happy driving two counties over to pay more fer the same thing now are they?

It troubles me Birch, but ya make a fair enough point.

I can tell ya Charlie, you'll be leavin' Jenny a damn sight better off, and it ain't like a state pension is gonna do much when you hang up that holster.

So, an agreement was struck and the Sheriff had worried about it every second of every day since.

Many years of stress had worn deep into the Sheriff and had left a sort of unpleasing permanent crooked expression on his face. He was about as jumpy a man as you could ever meet, "nervous in the service."

After he and Birch went in to business together, he never issued any citations, never arrested anyone. Usually he would just about shit his drawers at even the thought of pulling someone over.

If the Sheriff would have only drank a bottle or two of the beer he hauled in his trunk he might have actually enjoyed fifteen minutes of life, but just the smell of beer made him sick.

So for a few more years, life went on in Pike County, Ohio just as it had for quite a while. The war would end and America would roll on. On the other side of the Buckeye state, a new adventure was underway. It's almost amazing how paths overlap, paths that shouldn't even rub elbows.

Chapter 5, 1946 – On a train to the Windy City

Slowly opening his eyes, Bernard Hoffmiller realized he has drifted off to sleep for a few minutes as he is awakened by a noisy section of track. Half asleep, he gently rocks back and forth with the sounds of the track smacking loose ties as the train rolls through the countryside.

In the early fall of 1946 during his junior year at college, Bernard's friends convinced him to take a train from Cincinnati, Ohio to Chicago for several days of sightseeing and relaxation in the Windy City.

President Truman would officially end the war in several months and Americans were slowly and cautiously starting to enjoy life again.

Bernard had never been to a city larger than Dayton. He retrieved a suitcase from the open attic over the garage. The suitcase smelled slightly musty and carried the full range of odors from the garage. Leaving Preble County was something that didn't happen very much in the Hoffmiller family. Carefully packing several suits, Bernard was so eager about the trip he barely slept.

The next morning his father dropped Bernard and his pals from college off at the Union Station terminal in Cincinnati. They had left Eaton at 4:30 a.m. All of them dressed in their suits for traveling had ridden in the back of an old farm truck farm from outside of Eaton to Cincinnati.

Earlier in the morning Bernard's mother had swept out the truck bed and laid down a few clean quilts for their early morning ride.

It was a crisp morning, just cold enough to see your breath. As they made their way down the rolling hills of State Route 503, the boys could feel the sharp difference of the coolness in the air at the bottom of each hill and the warmth at the tops.

Bernard's father unloaded his payload of college boys, firmly shaking each of the boys' hands, telling each of them to mind their Ps & Qs in the big city. Each of the boys assured him they would and thanked him for the ride.

The train ride to Chicago was certainly exciting and relaxing; it was the longest train ride Bernard had ever taken and the farthest from home he had ever been.

The farms through Indiana seemed to all blend together. The land was beautiful, most of the crops had been taken in, and many of the fields were fall plowed and resting, it had been an early harvest. Bernard knew what crop had been in each field he passed, all of his boyhood was spent in the fields and he respected the farming way of life.

Farming had provided his family with a very comfortable existence in the worst of times. It was a hard life, the work never ended.

For miles and miles Bernard had noticed huge plumes of smoke.

What is that, he asked his friend Robert who was from South Bend?

Bernie that is the finest steel in the world, straight from Gary, Indiana! My boy they're making bridge trusses and beams for new sky scrapers so that we may continue to build our fine nation, and with this Bernard's friend held his arm high and toasted him with an imaginary glass.

Staring at a cute young lady and smiling from ear to ear Robert continued, this weekend we will celebrate the U S of A's return to domestic matters, hubba da hubba da hubba da!

As the train made its way through Gary, Indiana, Bernard was amazed at the size of the steel plants.

Soon, Chicago was coming into view. As the train stopped, Bernard was amazed as he looked around. Red caps everywhere, kids laughing, kids crying, hoards of people were walking in every direction, thousands of people, some smiling, some not, with thousands of destinations. It was overwhelming.

C'mon Bernie let's hit every joint in town!

No thanks, you gents enjoy yourselves, I am going to have some coffee and take in the sights I'll meet up with you at the hotel.

Bernard didn't really drink and he knew that being even slightly intoxicated was no way to enjoy a new city. Also being from Eaton, Ohio he knew that a drunken country boy in a strange city was never a good idea.

After walking with his suitcase in hand for a few hours in downtown Chicago, he decided that he not only wanted some coffee but perhaps some dinner, it was 8 p.m. The choices seemed endless as there were small kitchens everywhere, all appeared to be packed, and the smell of food was becoming irresistible. He stopped at the next place.

"To Each His Own" by the Ink Spots was playing when he walked in. The music was being played on-air and piped in from the radio station next door.

The place was packed, with barely room to walk. There were two empty stools at the counter. One was next to a rather large fellow who was already utilizing nearly half of the vacant space, and the other a tight corner. The corner it was.

Out from behind a diamond patterned stainless wall a lady with a blue and white check-plaid hat and matching apron appeared, Yah need a minute hun or aiR yah far sure ready?

What's good?

The lady pointed to the lighted list on the wall above and responded, it's all good or I wouldn't serve it, we're busy hun so what's it gonna be huh?

Fine, I'll have the Metropolitan steak on toast along with some mashed potatoes and gravy over all . . . oh and some grape jelly.

You got dat in a jiffy, the lady responded with a distinctly Chicagoan accent.

Just then the two seats next to Bernard became available and were immediately taken by two very attractive young ladies.

You shoulda got the chicken, one lady said to Bernard.

Pardon, replied Bernard.

You shoulda got the chicken, it's just da best.

Just then the other girl said: Hi, I am Vi and this is Kate, you got a name?

Yes, my name is Bernard.

You from Kentucky Bernard, asked Vi.

No I am NOT from Kentucky, why would you ask such a question?

No offense Bernie, but you sound like you're from Kentucky.

Well I am not, Bernard sternly replied. I am from Eaton Ohio, attending college at Miami University in Oxford.

So, how far is that from Kentucky, Kate asked?

Looking down at the counter and slightly shaking his head Bernard quietly responded, well obviously not far enough. While undetectable to him, Bernard was aware of the *Southern Ohio accent*.

The ladies busted out in laughter and so did Bernard, things became more relaxed. Vi switched places with Kate, so now she was setting next to Bernard.

Got a light Bernie?

I don't use tobacco.

With a flirty smugness Vi responds; Hey I didn't ask you for a stogie Bernie, just a light.

Bernard scrambled for the matches on the counter and quickly came to attention with one lit match in hand.

Violet leaned in and softly drew Bernard's hand to the end of her cigarette. He noticed how dark her eyes were and how blond her hair was, he couldn't help but smile. Violet returned that smile. So it was. Chicago ended up being much more than a train trip to the big city for a young man from Southwest Ohio.

As Bernard smiles and kisses a beautiful young Violet for the very first time in downtown Chicago, he realizes how happy he is that he did not join his pals who by now were certainly drunk. While they were slowly falling down in a bar a few miles away, he was rapidly falling in love.

Farm Boy and City Girl

Bernard grew up on a large farm in Preble County, Ohio just south of Eaton. His mother was a teacher at the local school and he and his father farmed the 400 acres that had been in his family for nearly seventy years.

Bernard was a stout young man at 6'1" and 200 pounds.

Life had always been good for the Hoffmiller family even at times when desperation was all around them.

Mr. Hoffmiller had really wanted one or even all of his boys to continue farming, with Bernard being the only child left he realized his dream would remain just that. He forgave his country for taking his two oldest sons in the Pacific Theater as he forgave his only remaining son for seeking out his own dream.

Bernard was the baby of the family and the only surviving child out of three boys; his two older brothers, Clarence and Teddy had been killed during the war in the very same week one year prior.

He would never forget the day his mother and father got the "visit" and found out about the death of his brothers. It was the day they both became eternally numb.

From that point forward their lives became a daily series of things to be done. They stopped even privately questioning their tasks and just did them. They moved into their own bedrooms for good. Their smiles, if any, were always quick, partial and strained. Their laughter forever contained. While completely unknown to them, they both wore their pain openly, and their pain wore into them openly, all the way to their soul.

Emotionally moving ahead would never be an option for the Hoffmiller's when two thirds of their life had been taken from them in one fateful day.

In the 1940s there was no one waiting for you in a nice room with expensive leather furniture and smelly never-to-be-lit candles explaining to you with a soft voice that loss is a part of life that must be accepted. Instead, the shock of a loved one's death tore through you until either it faded away or you faded away as a result, and that's how it was. In those days you didn't bullshit yourself into thinking you could actually negotiate the circumstance, whatever it may be. Life rolled on, with you or over you.

Violet Szakal was an only child from Chicago and had always lived in the city, only leaving to travel abroad with her eccentric parents. She had graduated from the Chicago School of Fine Arts. She had an unusual upbringing with a German Jewish father and a Hungarian Jewish mother. They were pacifists. They landed in the United States right after World War I. From a very early age they carefully crafted Violet's view of life. While privately being devoutly religious, they did not attend temple and they did not live in a traditional Jewish neighborhood. They didn't deny being Jews, but they certainly didn't advertise.

The Szakals lived in a beautiful brownstone surrounded by shops, eateries and people.

They were private people and they each respected the privacy and views of others. Love had brought them together, and love had kept them together.

Mrs. Szakal had worried since she found out where Violet and Bernard would be living. While dreading it, she finally approached Violet to discuss her upcoming married life.

Violet I want to discuss with you, your marriage to Bernard.

Yes, mother I knew this would happen, I know Bernard is a goy.

No, no, this has nothing to do with Bernard. It is his love for our daughter that is our only concern. I think Bernard is a fine man and a good man. I believe he is honest and your father and I love him like he is our son. But, I want you to consider with great care this remote place you are moving to in the state of Ohio.

Violet, you look and sound like a city Jew, do you know this?

Mother, please . . . I look and sound like Violet.

To you darling and to your friends, you are Vi. But my dear, you must understand that you dress, talk, have interests and even eat much differently than the people where you are going to live with your husband. This will not go un-noticed no matter what you do.

Do you know that where you are going to live is a known area for the hooded Klan purists? They hate Jews just as much as the colored. Never discuss your heritage, please promise me. You have never known hatred like this Violet, ignorant hatred without cause or justification.

Ima, have you not taught me that people are mostly good, and that tolerance of others is necessary for a peaceful life?

It is not your tolerance of others that worries me; there is no shiksa potion for you.

Oh, please.

Do you know that without even mentioning it, instead of butter these rural people will use swine renderings to make pies, pastries and cakes?

No, Ima I did not know that.

You will not be able to ask them, they will talk about you if you do. Have you been to this place?

No I have not, but Bernie has assured me that it is not much different than where he has grown up.

That does not comfort me, do you know where the closest temple is located, Dayton? Cincinnati?

Ima . . . please, I do not go to temple, I am not religious.

Perhaps dear, but you are still a Jew. A temple is always a safe place. You have been raised differently and I fear that you will realize this difference very soon. I beg you to consider my words, perhaps convince Bernard of a different setting for your new life. Your father and I will fully support both of you if Bernard would like to establish himself here.

I know he would not consider that. I think things will be just fine.

Also, please do not pick up the "new" Bible, please.

I will not Ima.

Violet, please know that you cannot come home to live once you are married just because you are unhappy. Your father and I agree about this.

Not fully understanding her Mother's fears, Violet is excited thinking about her new life.

Violet was a clay artist; she loved to sculpt and to create things from clay. While some of her art was a bit advanced for the day, some would even say suggestive, Violet didn't care. The exotic curves created by her hands in clay were her view of the curves of life.

1948 had been a good year, the war was over and things were really starting to improve across the nation. After nearly two years traveling back and forth and sending countless letters, Violet and Bernard were married. Bernard announced that he was officially never going to sleep or otherwise on a davenport in Chicago again.

They had only been married a few weeks and on June the second, nineteen hundred and forty eight they were on their way to Hillsboro, Ohio to make their new home.

Bernard had accepted a position as an assistant bank manager at the Hillsboro Savings and Loan, in Hillsboro, Ohio. While somewhat remote, the bank was a major money center in this part of Southern Ohio. A large amount of money flowed in at the fall harvest, and a large amount of money flowed out at planting time. Burley tobacco was becoming a major crop and it generated a great deal of money in the area.

Motoring down Ohio State Route 50 in Bernard's new 1948 Hudson Commodore Eight, they held their hands out in the wind and loudly sang songs replacing the words they didn't remember.

There hadn't been very many new cars produced for a few years because of the war. Bernard's parents had purchased the car for him as a wedding and college graduation present.

This was the first car Bernard had ever seen with a built in radio. He tuned in WLW from Cincinnati hoping to treat Violet to the beautiful voices of one or both of the Clooney sisters; instead the Reds were tied up with the St. Louis Cards, four innings deep.

As Bernard and Violet approached Hillsboro, a house like neither of them had ever seen was coming into view on the top of hill near the edge of town, it was a beautiful home that seemed so out of place for the area after miles and miles of tobacco barns. The home was owned by the artist, Hollis Westland. Violet had heard of Westland and was familiar with his work. Bernard had enquired about the unusual house during his interview with the bank.

Westland created artwork on paper and from clay and metal. All of his pieces were what most would call *art nouveau*.

Mrs. Violet Hoffmiller

I assumed that Hillsboro was going to be no worse than Eaton, for God sakes that ended up being wishful thinking. I wanted to move home to Chicago so bad. When we first looked for a place to live, I was so depressed that I begged Bernie not to move here. I lost - ultimately we lost. But it took a while.

God I tried, I tried to do everything I could. I tried to be what my parents had told me I should.

There was no place to get an espresso coffee in this town; there were no galleries or Ladies shops. The only bakery was terrible, no bagels, no rye. Just wet crust pies and bland or stale everything else. The people in this town appeared to live on their front porch, door always open. I had never seen anything like this.

The community was overflowing in misinformation about almost everything.

Clusters of little busybody mothers walked the streets with their broods in tow, all in training to be ignorant walking talking rumor mills. Their mouths were always open even if nothing was being said. From humble white lie beginnings to an outrageous life-destroying event, a conjured story could travel from one end of the town to the other in a single afternoon. This happened every day.

A new victim was always available. The stares these people would cast - the things they would say - were almost unreal. I could hardly listen; I would just roll my eyes, silently curse, and move on.

There was no way I could engage these people in any sort of conversation as that would have been impossible. I could not believe how different the people were, I would never understand them. They never discussed anything real, anything that mattered. These people were still blaming Negroes for everything possible.

While only 350 miles from Chicago, I could have just as easily been in China, in fact it may have been better because I would not have understood what I was hearing.

We found a house in town that was within our budget at 26 N. Mulberry St.

The door creaked open and the gas fireplace was immediately in view. The house smelled like old newspapers. The tattered drapes that remained on the windows looked as old as the house.

The stairway was an L stairway with a small landing with a large window half the way up. This window overlooked the entire town. The bathroom had a huge gas-fired hot water tank in one corner. The house certainly needed some work, but it was welcoming and very well designed.

Southern Ohio was an odd place. Hillsboro was wretched from the start. Everyone seemed to know your business well before you did. There were no secrets except those waiting to be made up about you by the locals. They were terrible to each other, and newcomers were under a microscope of unbelievable resolution.

While moving in, one person came to investigate toting a basket of fresh biscuits and homemade jam, Ms. Margie Makintosh. She was what the locals called a "granny woman."

I had never heard this term. She explained to me that she would help deliver babies, teach women to nurse properly, and clean out and stitch up wounds.

Ms. Makintosh was never married and had lived with her brother Anthony and her sister-in-law, Esther all of her life. They had both passed away and she now lived alone. Margie was lonely and she would stay all night if not shooed off.

Eventually she would privately confess to me that she preferred the company of a woman and that she would love the comfort of an older woman companion.

Over time I would also find that she would rush to the door with any bad news for you, but any good news, compliments or tales of victory were not relayed with the same enthusiasm if mentioned at all. It seemed this was the way of everyone in Hillsboro. These people craved disaster while trampling on every four leaf clover they could find.

Bernard was a Methodist and I was a non-practicing Jew. I didn't care about religion, faith yes, religion no. I had a difficult time with the Old Testament; the New Testament was completely unacceptable. For me a church or temple was not a sanctuary for good, it was instead a restrictive place to insure a restricted life fashioned by the person behind the pew.

God had created a violent earth, with violent creatures, the most violent of all being man.

All through known history men had killed each other for any and all reasons, while claiming they were all serving God, some God.

While I was grateful for life and my own existence, I could never imagine a God who would insist on continual praise from a creature as insignificant as myself. I could never imagine a God who would allow such unchecked suffering in the world only to reward the forgiven and supposed faithful with eternal joy. This was a "club" I could never join.

I told Bernard before we were married that I would not pray as he did, I would not bow to his "Son of God" and that I would never get on my knees in a church, take Communion, sing, etc.

Still, we tried to occasionally attend the First United Methodist church, but like everything else that was Hillsboro, rumors and less than flattering stares made Sunday mornings very unpleasant.

Bernard insisted that we attend, it was our place in the community that he was most concerned about. It was his place in my heart that I was most concerned about.

Several months had passed and I convinced Bernard to purchase a potter's wheel and large gas kiln. I missed working with clay, I missed my art.

Many of my pieces were abstract compilations. I would try to combine shapes from nature and the human anatomy, finishing with glazes of my own creation. I experimented with many textures and colors.

To Bernard's dismay, I started to display my pieces along our walkway and porch. I would listen to the hateful and painful comments of the people who walked by. I was stunned and hurt, but my motivation was unaffected.

Many times I would find that my pieces would get damaged or destroyed overnight or while we were away. I had decided that the more my art would be vandalized, the more erotic it would become.

If this was war, and it was, I was not going to back down. So I created a masterpiece. It was a large fountain vase standing nearly two feet tall, in the shape of a single breast with one perfect nipple shape, glazed with a perfect "titty pink." It was spectacular. The nipple had a small hole perfectly in the center for a fountain.

I fitted the pump and filled "her" up for the trial. It work perfectly, the nipple shot a perfect stream nearly two feet to the catch basin to be recirculated. I put indigo blue coloring in the water reserve and the result was just spectacular.

Bernard arrived home from the bank and he was furious.

Violet! Is it your intention to see that we are forcefully removed from this town? Shall I just resign my position at the bank rather than wait for an embarrassing discharge due to my wife's suggestive so called *art* display?

Violet, darling, there must be some limits here. I realize this is your artwork, but a large breast that squirts blue water placed next to the sidewalk? This is not Paris darling, or even Chicago, this is southern Ohio in case I need to remind you.

You will never convince me that you could have displayed a large breast squirting blue water in Chicago.

Bernard was right, this was retaliatory. It brought unnecessary attention to us.

I had begun to shut it off and move it when a small crowd gathered and the town was already buzzing with hateful rumors.

A county deputy sheriff showed up and insisted the fountain was immoral and threatened to destroy it, unless I covered it and took it immediately in the house.

The Deputy was not kind: Sir and Madam either remove this item from public view NOW and keep it in your home or I will remove it from public view for good.

As it happened, Mr. Hollis Westland had driven by and seen the fountain during the fiasco. He later sent his man to enquire about the fountain and he offered me $1,000 for its acquisition. His man was a small Asian fellow that had been his secret companion for years, his name was Marion. I initially refused to sell my fountain, but I was convinced that it may be an opportunity to meet Mr. Westland.

Marion had also convinced me when he said it is better to "have profit from my art than see it destroyed by hillsbully."

A few days after agreeing to sell the fountain, I received an embossed invitation for tea from Mr. Westland. I responded and couldn't wait to meet him. Bernard was not at all keen on the idea.

I remember ringing his door chime.

Mr. Westland answered the door, ah Violet, hello my dear lady, come in, come in, do I detect a Chicagoan, what I wouldn't give for a large hamburg sandwich from Hackney's!

Yes, Chicagoan for sure! I would love to join you for a sandwich at Hackney's.

Perhaps we shall darling, perhaps we shall. I assume that you are ready to go home and escape the wretched beasts of this Southern Ohio asylum?

Oh yes, the next train, bus or mule cart!

We both laughed.

Violet darling, do not allow the beauty of this area to be spoiled by the insanity of the local minds that inhabit it. While I do not forgive these people for their ignorant acts and horrible discussions, I never forget that their imprisonment in this area has stripped them of the ability to be human or humane.

They wallow with each other in so much ignorance that it could never be washed off completely.

Mr. Westland then smiled and said; or to be blunt, the smell of fresh shit will never be fully disguised by Lavender water or muted with Gin darling.

I chuckled, my God . . . it is so nice to hear someone verbalize my every thought. Oh, Mr. Westland, I feel so out of place and so starved of what I thought was real.

Call me Hollis dear, first names please . . . Perched on this hill I look out and see the beauty of this area without hearing the voices or seeing the mouths speak that would be certain to ruin it for me. It is a calm I can and do enjoy.

So tell me dear Violet, what has brought this pretty young sophisticate here?

I explained that I met Bernard in Chicago and that we had moved here as a result of Bernard securing a position at the bank.

Hollis interrupted, was this breast modeled after one of your own ladies.

Rather embarrassed, I admitted this as true.

Immediately Mr. Westland clapped his hands and spoke in Chinese to his man, asking for his wallet.

Violet darling, every afternoon at exactly 3 p.m. you will hear Marion lifting the magical arms of several aluminum ice trays so that we may enjoy the most delicious of chilled alcoholic concoctions, please join us.

Mr. Westland and I became loving friends, and I did join Hollis and Marion nearly every day. However in a town like Hillsboro, this did not go unnoticed.

"Well there she goes, up to service her old rich man" was one of the kinder comments circulating about me.

On a Tuesday afternoon right before I would have normally made the trek to The Westland home, I received a strange call from the Church Deacon.

The phone rang and I answered:

Hello.

Yes, Mr. Hoffmiller, please.

This is Violet, Mrs. Hoffmiller.

This is Deacon Wermire and the Pastor would like to confer with Mr. Hoffmiller tonight at 6:30 p.m.

As I was trying to confirm and say good bye, the deacon rudely hung up.

At exactly 6:30 p.m. Bernard and I welcomed the pastor into our home. He refused to sit down.

He would only address Bernard outside, so they walked into the backyard. I listened at the kitchen window as I glared at the pastor through the screen.

The Pastor began:

This is a sad day for me Mr. Hoffmiller, but the congregation has been made aware of what at the least could be described as an unsavory relationship between your wife and that kook of a Hollis Westland.

As well, it has been brought to our attention that your wife is a Jew. We have no place in our church for an unholy Jew or her gentile husband.

If that's not enough Mr. Hoffmiller, the supposed works of clay art created by your Mrs. Hoffmiller go well beyond what anyone could consider decent or useful.

Not vessels for food or drink, instead gross exaggerations of the human anatomy, unholy shapes with unholy purposes displayed as if they serve some purpose for our Lord.

Bernard turned purple and I immediately started clapping, crying and screaming at the Pastor, "Good, that's good pastor because this 'Jew' who is obviously little more than an unholy WHORE doesn't want to be in your dammed church worshipping your dammed son of god, relying on a false new bible that was re-written by a corrupt King for a corrupt purpose.

Who is Satan's father Pastor? Tell me OH great pious man, who is Satan's father?   As I suspected, you will not answer will you Pastor?   But we share something in common. Like you, my savior is also a JEW but his name isn't Jesus, his name is Albert Einstein and he has saved us all, yes pastor one JEW saved your ass and mine . . . . . . Leave my yard schmeckel."

The pastor quickly left. Bernard did not utter a word to me.

Chapter 6, A Non-traditional Family

Bernie and I lived in Hillsboro for several years. We tried many times to conceive a child, but it just wasn't to be.

Perhaps it was not being able to conceive a child; perhaps it was just my appearance, or God forbid old Mr. Westland.

I was a shapely woman and men in this community were so eagerly kind, this did not go unnoticed. Bernard was incredibly jealous of me, at times it destroyed him. He acted as if I was continually doing something wrong, he just seemed to be irritated at my very presence.

After many weeks and months I could no longer tolerate the continued tension that had built up in our relationship. I expressed myself completely and without regret.

"Bernard has it really been that bad? Has it been so entirely devastating that my love and kindness for you is just a veil that certainly must be hiding something wrong? If so, I am not the wife for you. It pains me to say that because I love you so much. But I can't be distracted by having to explain every second of my existence. I shouldn't have to explain anything to someone who I have expressed my complete love to.

You will trust me as I will trust you, and you will be confident that things are okay and so will I. Continually satisfying your insecurity wastes a tremendous amount of time Bernard, it's becoming obvious to our families and even to this wretched community, it's embarrassing.

Bernard darling, jealously rapidly drains the love out of our relationship as the gutter drains the rain. Do you see this, and do you understand these made up feelings that loom in your mind only harm us?

No benefit is derived Bernard.

Shall I flatten my tits and shave off my hips and my ass? Shall I remain a recluse in this house, wearing nothing that conforms to the curves of my body? Will you still find me attractive and do you wish me to be seen only in unstylish and ill-fitting baggy clothes? Perhaps just a feed-sack?"

Amid the shouts and empty accusations, a fragile peace developed, it was not to last.

Bernard always fell back on the same statement which was, "I can't make you happy no matter what I do."

To which I would respond, "You know who says that Bernard, someone who hurts a person's feelings and then wants to act as if he is the victim, instead of the person perpetuating the situation."

Again and again we had these same arguments over nothing, again and again I was accused of the most outrageous things. I was growing numb, I wanted to go home so desperately. I secretly begged my parents to allow me to come home and they would not. It was so awful that I begged Bernard to hit me, I begged him for a reason to leave, he would not oblige.

Finally I asked, "Bernard darling is our intent in this relationship to only dissect that which we do not understand about each other? Or should we accept our differences and strengthen that which bonds us?"

In time the accusations turned to occasional grumbles, and grumbles turned to silence - continual silence.

For months only the most necessary of conversation was had. My only peace, my only hope was my art.

I had developed an excellent friendship with Hollis, whom I cared for very deeply. Not in a lover's way but as an older brother or father.

He encouraged my patience with Bernard and helped me to refine my art. He was my only dear friend in what I had now termed: "Hell's-boro."

I know the locals had their wicked fun, accusing Mr. Westland of taking me for wheelchair rides around his mansion while setting on his lap. In truth, Mr. Westland could barely navigate his wheel chair with himself aboard. I was supposedly his "special nurse."

While I did help care for Mr. Westland, it was out of kindness and nothing else. He had confessed to me that he was a homosexual, which I had actually known from the first time we met. Growing up in the city, I knew the signs, the look and the subtle expressions of a homosexual male. I also knew that in Hillsboro, Ohio a homosexual would be considered a pedophile, so my lips were sealed.

Finally, I had convinced Bernie of considering adoption when we had heard about the special brothers being raised by a local church. Bernard was very much against adopting the boys.

We had both heard many rumors about the boys in town. Supposedly they were *possessed*; supposedly they had *powers*. I found them adorable and in need of our love.

Hugh and Ursal would seldomly talk, but they seemed to have a special way of communicating with each other.

I could tell the boys were extremely reliant on facial expressions. By how you looked they could nearly guess what you were going to say - they didn't need to talk. On Sundays the boys would be rolled to the front of the congregation like human props to hold the collection plates as they would return to the Alter.

The pastor hadn't engaged the boys in conversation; instead he and his son sternly cared for the boys like two caged dogs. Oddly enough the boys could recite an entire Sunday service word for word, including the pastor's not-so-religious comments on the weekly tithe once the congregation had left.

Each time a person would enter or leave the church or asked to be saved, both boys would go into action.

"Quarter in," said Ursal.

"Quarter out," said Hugh.

"A gift for the lord," said Ursal

"Praise god almighty," said Hugh

Over and over the boys would recite this over and over, *quarter in, quarter out, quarter in, quarter out.*

Hugh had a speech impediment and that added to the comical aspect of their recitals.

Hugh and Ursal would take turns rapidly repeating the Pastors entire sermon. They worked in unison so well that it was almost as if they were a synchronized recording machine, each at perfect timing reciting the sermon a line or two at a time, never overlapping one another.

Sometimes the Pastor would become so enraged that he would strike the boys and knock them out of their old wicker wheel chairs to the floor. They would scurry to their knees and quickly hold hands and loudly scream a prayer, bobbing up and down in unison:

Father God, father God, father God, who's only son is Jesus, please kill this man please kill this unholy man for hitting the brothers who are bowed only for you Lord.

Then the boys would recite and act out God's answer with a loud southern Ohio accent.

"Fear not," said Ursal.

"Yes, yes my lord say more, say more," said Hugh. "The Lord hears you and will cast evil from this earth and this place."

"Yes, thank you my Lord, *kill him, kill him*," said Hugh.

The boys would get *the spirit* and talk in tongues with the most heinous of requests. They would repeat things over and over as they screamed and whaled out bobbing up and down on their knees in a fit, eyes closed and crying. It was a surreal spectacle. The pastor would become so enraged that with closed fist he would hit the boys so hard that they would sometimes be knocked unconscious.

He would then lock the boys in the basement and they would continue this ritual day and all night sometimes for three days straight.

When either Pastor Williams or his son would finally open the basement door, there the boys would be on their knees together, holding hands and squinting while looking at the open door after setting in total darkness, having pissed and shit themselves, puking from the smell and raw from setting in all of it, yet never saying a word in complaint.

The boys were driving the already insane Pastor and his family to the breaking point. Normal could no longer be defined or reached, if it ever had.

The boys RAPIDLY recited the pastors favorite sermon and tongue talking: *The Lord Jesus Christ, yes yes…abu abu lom do o lomo, the Lord Jesus Christ . . . Is coming, Is coming, to retrieve his flock . . . yes yes, claim the children of Christ . . . oh praise God, taking his babies from this evil earth, praise him, oh Father God, Father God, coming to claim his followers and destroy those who stand against Christ.*

During the adoption process, Pastor Williams asked Bernard and me if we had accepted the Lord Jesus Christ as our Savior.

Bernard replied that our religious beliefs should bear no relevance in the decision regarding the boys.

The Pastor lashed out, "The Lord will strike down those who stand against Jesus Christ and reward those who follow our savior, Father God, AAAmen."

After the adoption was complete and we finally had the boys at home to stay for a few days, I became aware of an unusual anatomical issue with both boys while bathing them and I screamed and nearly passing out.

The boys didn't appear to have any testicles, and barely a scrotum. I was so immediately upset that I trembled and I could barely contain myself.

The boys were upset.

What's wong wif mame Ursal? Is it sin wemoved (removed)?

Alarmed, I quickly called the Pastor, I was crying and in complete shock.

While waiting for the Pastor to answer the phone, Hugh tried to comfort me saying; it's sin wemoved mame, for me and Ursal mame, for me and Ursal it's sin wemoved.

I was nearly hysteric and I slowly thought I was starting to understand the situation. I hung up the phone while sinking to the floor in tears.

What did you say Hugh, what did you say?

He said, "sin wemoved mame."

So you mean Pastor Williams did this to you, he did this to you?

Yes mame, he said that we should have sin wemoved and not be like the whore gurl who was our first mame, so he took our marbles.

I was spinning, and I cried uncontrollably. I was very familiar with the practice of circumcision; I was not familiar with complete sterilization.

I called Bernard at work and told him to come home immediately. Bernard arrived home and examined the boys. We both wept as the boys watched not really knowing what had happened to them earlier in life.

Bernard had not seen the boys nude and the only male I had ever seen nude was Bernard. I didn't know what a small boy's scrotum should look like; I barely knew what an adult male scrotum looked like.

It's not as if you would even think about asking to see a child nude during the adoption process - that would end the possibility of adoption on the spot.

We decided that we had to get the boys to a real doctor. We all quickly piled in the car and headed for Cincinnati, finding a Dr. Baumritter in the phone directory that would immediately see the boys.

The dimly lit office smelled of alcohol and bandages.

After what seemed like hours, we were called for the boys to be examined.

We explained to the doctor that we had recently adopted the boys only becoming aware of the situation after the adoption. Disgusted, he told us that while the practice in his opinion was inhumane, it was not illegal as far as he knew. In fact, Ohio's neighbor Indiana had laws supporting the sterilization of "feebleminded" children and adults.

"The treatment of children as farm animals even mentally disturbed children is beyond my ability to understand. In all likelihood these boys will still be able to achieve an erection; they may still be able to engage in coitus."

Dr. Baumritter called Pastor Williams in our presence, he confirmed he had done the "lords work" but would say no more.

Go home folks, just go home. There is nothing I can do for you. The boys appear healthy and the damage is done. Perhaps seek legal counsel and pursue the matter in court.

On the way home I begged Bernard to leave.

Bernie please darling, let's leave this place. I will go anywhere, we can move to Eaton and you can farm.

I will do anything to get out of this place. I hate it here, I hate it.

Unfortunately, Bernard would not consider moving.

What we would ultimately learn is that the good Pastor Williams had seen fit to remove the boy's testicles in his office with no anesthetic; crudely stitching they're young and now devoid of sin scrotums.

Of course his work was for the Lord. The boys would have certainly sinned with these testicles, so that sin had to be preemptively removed; it was God's wish. It was the work of the Lord. I simply could not believe it.

Bernard immediately hired one of the larger law firms in Cincinnati to file suit against Pastor Williams. There had to be some punishment for the man who had basically chopped the testicles off of two little boys who were already so pitiful.

As horrific as the first days were with the boys, they were obviously resilient and very funny. We enjoyed their antics. They would role-play Pastor Williams's past arguments with his wife, one being the wife and the other the pastor. Even though it was a bit spooky at times, it was usually just hilarious.

Hugh was the comical one and the more curious of the two, always asking me, "What's the secwet of wife mame, pwease whats the secwet tell me again?"

To which I would always respond, Where there can be life there will be life Hugh.

"Did Gosh tell this mame, did Gosh say this with you?"

It's not Gosh Hugh, it's God, and no he didn't tell me this but he has shown me this wherever I may look on this earth. God speaks only with his actions dear, not with his voice, just as we sometimes should.

My parents had told me this all of my life, and I thought that it bore repeating, especially considering all that the boys had experienced in their young lives.

The charges against Pastor Williams were soon made public; the entire town was under a cloud. Most folks sided with the good pastor and his family, not believing the heinous medical procedure alleged in the legal case was wrong. However Pastor Williams's congregation numbers had slipped and the twisted word of God was becoming a lot less profitable.

Bernard worked and we stayed at home.

We had a few friends who loved to stop by just to hear the boys recite the pastors past services in unison, especially the pastors private comments after church services.

For being so obviously disadvantaged, the boys just seemed to remember everything. It was obvious they were special. They could communicate with each other without uttering a sound.

The Trial

All rise, The Honorable Judge John Michael Wadson presiding.

Please be seated, bailiff call the accused to stand before this court.

Mr. John Williams.

That's Pastor Williams.

MR. WILLIAMS, this court is not concerned with your pastoral activities, are you or are you not Mr. John Williams?

Yes, I am PASTOR John Williams.

Then please stand silent while the charges against you are read aloud.

The trial began. Lawyers probed deep into Pastor Williams past.

John Williams takes the stand:

The lawyer asks the Pastor about his time at medical school. The Pastor states that he was called to serve the lord and quit medical school as it went against the teachings of Christ.

Testimony begins:

Pastor Williams aside from the grotesque procedure you performed on these boys, who were you to decide to remove their later reproductive abilities?

I did not.

You didn't perform the procedure, the botched and evil surgical procedure on these young boys?

The all mighty hand of God decided that these boys, these here boys should not have the ability to sin. The court of God is the true court of man, you will never win in God's court.

The crowd roared and the judge broke the gavel insisting silence.

Finally order was restored.

You may continue counsel.

Pastor Williams, is any cause so just as to kill or maim a child - child in your care, solely dependent on you for any and all care that the child would receive?

The work of the Lord, needn't be justified to man or this court.

The Lord's hands did not perform this gross operation; you did this Pastor Williams, at your discretion and without medical training and justification.

Prior to beginning litigation, I had asked Bernard many times how we would define a victory against the pastor. What would be fair? He knew the Pastor would never be imprisoned for this, he knew the Pastor had nothing in the way of possessions. The only thing the pastor had was an insane mind that had somehow justified a lifetime of insane actions, and a pitiful family that mindlessly followed him, never capable of pondering other choices.

The trial dragged on.

Motions and counter motions were filed, piles of meaningless documents that regardless of their content, truth or otherwise, would do nothing to change the boys lives or any lives for the better. In fact, things would only get worse.

Months passed and finally Pastor Williams was found guilty only of lying about performing the procedure. We received nothing. The pastor had nothing.

This had been an expensive nightmare with nothing gained, only time and money lost. Hugh and Ursal could never be made whole. Instead we had filled the bank account of a large law firm, period.

Bernard and I were so depressed and so disgusted. We learned a very valuable and expensive lesson. Before embarking on anything of a legal nature in the future, we would insist that a goal be defined with absolute clarity about what the potential outcomes would be. If we could not confidently define a favorable outcome, we would not take the chance and allow one to be defined for us.

Life with Hugh and Ursal

The boys had learned to hobble around very well. They were allowed to walk everywhere in town. Each of the boys wore leg braces on both legs as they had not developed normally due to rickets.

Hugh and Ursal were hard to define. In some ways they were certainly handicapped; however neither could be considered ignorant. In fact, they were very cunning and quite shrewd.

Everywhere they would go, they would always hold hands. If other children would make fun of them, they would drop to their knees wherever they were at and pray loudly and in unison. This would literally stop people in their tracks, not just because of what they were doing but what they were saying.

The boys would pray for people to die or to be harmed in some other way, no one had ever heard or seen anything like it. The boys commanded respect; hell they were revered by most people and the locals just tried to avoid them at all costs.

They would stand holding hands looking and listening in front of houses and businesses or even the courthouse.

They couldn't see very well, but they could hear a pin drop with a train pulling into town, and they did hear . . . everything from everyone. They knew every secret in town, even those that people thought well kept.

On one Tuesday afternoon many months after adopting the boys Bernard arrived home not to the normal cheerful greeting at the door with the smells of dinner escaping from the Kitchen; instead, I was cleaning the bathroom on my hands and knees and the house smelled of smoke.

Bernard dear, the bathroom caught fire today . . . from . . . under the hot water tank, Bernard was puzzled.

Darling if you require seductive nudity, and the most perfect and pointed of all pointy bosoms . . . and since we are legally married, perhaps I could assist you, rather than risking burning the house down . . . Bernard was even more puzzled.

Several hours earlier I had discovered smoke pouring from out of the bathroom. It appeared the large gas powered hot water tank had caught the floor on fire. After grabbing a large bucket of water and dousing the flames, I discovered a charred stack of seductive magazines that had been ignited by the burner.

In truth, the boys had found a box of discarded girly magazines inside an old garage in town and they were quite captivated by the material. In fact, they were so captivated that they rolled up every magazine they could carry, carefully inserting them down the sleeves of their coats, barely leaving room for their arms. They then decided that the best hiding place for the coveted material was under the hot water tank in the bathroom.

Unfortunately they had not considered the proximity of the open air burner to the *steamy* ignition source.

Fortunately, most of the smoke went up and out of the hot water tank flue and the bathroom and home were spared complete incineration.

The Big House on the Big Hill

Mr. Westland had been sick for months. Alcoholism and diabetes had finally taken their toll on my dear friend and removed the remaining life from this wonderful man. Aside from Marion, I was his only beneficiary.

Bernard was initially furious and I finally confessed to him that Mr. Westland was strictly a homosexual who would have never enjoyed any romantic interest in a woman.

Hollis had left a long letter for both Bernard and I where he described his gift not as a home to just live but as a sanctuary to escape the lunacy of the area and the stresses of life.

We slowly moved in, with Bernard initially dragging his heels the entire time. Once empty, Bernard sold our home for $600 more than the remaining value of the note.

Mr. Westland had also left over $50,000 in his safe for us. It was very much unexpected and we appreciated it greatly. Bernard slowly started to understand that Hollis was a good man and this pleased me.

The Westland house was simply beautiful. The house looked different from the many times I had visited before. Knowing someone had given this to me had made the house seem ever more special than it already was.

No expense had been spared in its construction. It was beautifully designed with six bedrooms. There were five bathrooms that were all tiled from floor to walls and ceiling.

It contained eight fireplaces, four of which could be operated on gas. A vast amount of valuable art remained.

Mr. Westland had designed his own special air conditioning system from a design he had seen in Italy. He contracted an Italian company to make the system on site, pouring large concrete slabs that were seven feet long and six feet wide and high.

Theses slabs contained coils of large diameter copper pipe. These were lowered into a large pond that was at least five hundred feet from the house. Water from these slabs was slowly pumped to the house via underground pipes. It would circulate into a special room in the basement where large fans would blow across coils of copper that were inside and this would cool the entire house.

It took the Italian crew nearly six months to complete the work. Mr. Westland had cared for the men very well while they were in the states, having special meals prepared for the men every day and entertaining them, showing movies every night.

The light tan stucco exterior with deep rust colored window frames and woodwork made the house look like a Mediterranean villa. The home, barns and outbuildings, the glass and every detail possible was impeccable.

Hollis had lived a very flamboyant life with friends spread around the globe. Hugh and Ursal found chest after chest full of costumes, foreign military uniforms from France, Italy and Germany, movie props, etc.

We also found a working movie projector and many old movies including Charlie Chaplin's "The Great Dictator" which the boys dearly loved. Marion had left all of their artwork hanging on the walls in the house.

Month after month we found something new. Living on the hill was indeed peaceful and for the first time in our married life Bernard and I were truly happy.

We made passionate love every day that it was possible and in all of my life I had never been so fulfilled. Our lives had improved, we felt purposed and we both brimmed with gratefulness and happiness.

For the first time and the only time, my parents visited us and my mother cooked Letcho, rye bread and so many wonderful dishes that after three weeks I was almost unable to wear some of my dresses. I was so sad to see them go home. It was the last time I would see my father alive.

As I would sit in the courtyard overlooking the valley, I missed my dear friend Hollis. I missed his wisdom and his words; I missed his presence and the warmth he provided to my soul. I thanked him repeatedly and I imagined him telling me, that I was welcomed and to enjoy my life.

Chapter 7, Money for Whom

As with everything in this life; my happiness was about to change. Bernard had been unexpectedly promoted and he had received a very large cash bonus. We were both shocked, and cautiously grateful.

As it would turn out, disaster lurked.

Several weeks later, on a Monday at 3 p.m. Bernard arrived home from work unusually early. He was obviously shaken and he appeared to be crying. He feared what is to come.

Bernard had been fired and the bank was accusing him of embezzlement.

The timing of the inheritance could not have been worse for us.

The next week Bernard was formally charged. He was arrested and jailed.

I drove with the boys to Columbus, Ohio to retain an attorney. It took over two weeks before the court would hold a hearing and set bail. The bail amount was set very high at $10,000 cash.

When Bernard had accepted his position at the bank, his manager, James McCabe who was the bank vice president had required that Bernard grant him complete Power of Attorney. He had told Bernard this was a necessary requirement so that he could conduct official business in Bernard's absence for example vacations, illness, etc. Bernard assumed this was a normal requisite and never questioned it. Bernard had no copy of the Power of Attorney he had signed, assuming it was on file with the county and the bank.

He was mistaken.

It appeared that Mr. McCabe had established accounts in Bernard's name at more than 10 different banks across the United States.

For more than three years now he had made cash deposits to each of those accounts all totaling more than $350,000 dollars.

He had skimmed the cash when paying out large farm loans in the spring and from large cash deposits during harvest each fall. Mysteriously all of the accounts had been emptied. A $1,500 check was cashed by Mr. McCabe acting as if he was Bernard. This was Bernard's cash bonus which wasn't from the bank at all.

Bernard was devastated. He had never lied or taken a dishonest penny from anyone, now facing a long prison sentence for crimes he did not commit.

Bernard would never be the same. He stayed home and would not leave the house. He lost more than 25 pounds in less than three months.

Over and over again he repeated his apology to me for not leaving Hillsboro and moving to Eaton or anywhere else as an alternative.

Things looked bad for us. It appeared obvious to the locals that Bernard had done what he was accused of. How were we living so well without receiving any income from Bernard's former position?

Bernard was a broken man, and I was his broken wife.

I could offer no words to comfort or console him. I could do nothing to change the blank expression of complete desperation that he would continually wear.

He stopped shaving, and bathing and his nails grew long and he smelled. Bernard was seriously ill. He felt so cheated, he was so enraged. He would scream loudly and with great fury with no one listening except himself.

I was so down, so low, that I could barely take care of myself and the boys. While the boys realized in part what was happening, they couldn't possibly understand the overall implications that we faced.

I would drive to neighboring communities for food and all other needed items. I would avoid Hillsboro at all costs. When I did drive through town people would tilt their heads back mocking me behind the wheel, acting as if we were all rich criminals.

Upon arriving home one afternoon, I knew something was different, something had happened . . . something I suspected would happen.

I was right, Bernard was dead.

He had shot himself in the barn while appearing to attempt the cleaning of a gun.

In truth, Bernard had never shot or cleaned a gun in his life that I was aware of; he despised violence of any sort. As upset as I was, I would never mention this to the insurance agent for the company who held his life insurance policy.

Again, the town was filled with rumors. I was initially accused of murdering my husband. I certainly felt that Bernard was murdered, indirectly by a Mr. McCabe.

Bernard was posthumously convicted of embezzlement and the court tried to seize the property that was left solely to me. I previously cleaned out the safe and hidden all of the money Hollis had left for us in several bread tins in places that no one would ever find. I managed to retain the property and all of the cash I had hidden.

All of Bernard's life insurance was revoked by the court and I would never receive a dime of money from his policy.

My husband may have had his faults, but he was always honest. He would have never cheated or stolen anything from anyone.

He cared about people, he cared about fairness. Yet an entire community had decided that he was a bad and unlawful man, a complex and educated thief. Never pondering why a man would educate himself and move to this God forsaken place for the sole purpose of defrauding people.

Had it not been for the boys I would have joined Bernard in the ground. The cold musty earth seemed like a welcoming place compared to the darkness where I now resided.

I felt as if I had little to live for. I was numb, I was damaged. I drank excessively and I enjoyed being drunk.

I had $67,000 in cash and I knew that with careful management, that amount of money would last a very long time. I didn't dare open an account anywhere. I realized that I would be under the watchful eye for the rest of my life.

As the months wore on and time passed, my drinking slowed down immensely. When I was alone, I would actually start to look at myself again, not as a damaged soul, but as a human being. While catching occasional glimpses, I would briefly and cautiously smile at myself in the mirror.

After months and months of self-pity, I was starting to understand that I was not dead, I was alive. I searched for a purpose. I started to create pottery again. Finally while thinking of Hollis mocking poor Marion's Asian accent while describing a nasty sexual act, I laughed and cried and laughed some more. I laughed so hard that I nearly pissed down my leg. It was as if an emotional dam had finally crumbled and my mind and my body had decided to rejoin and again become a functioning system.

I reached a point where I could again define who and what I was to myself. I had forgotten how important these thoughts were.

I would no longer waste time on remorse or plotting horrible and revengeful acts that I could never carry out.

I sat in the courtyard by myself and I remembered meeting Bernard in Chicago and his funny little accent. I remembered how serious he could be and how shy he was. I craved him so desperately, just to feel his breath on my face, to feel his hand upon my body. Just to hear him say, "I love you my darling" one final time.

I remembered how handsome he was and the first time that we made love on the davenport at my parents. I loved Bernard so dearly and I truly hoped that while he was still alive, he realized how much I loved him.

Life with Bernard had not always been easy, but it was our life and our short time together, it was all the time in this world that we would ever have together.

It would have been ungrateful and dishonest if only for the sake of continued mourning that I would not admit to myself how much I loved the beautiful man that had been my dear husband.

Chapter 8, I am Needed Again

I was educating Hugh and Ursal at home. They would have never survived a day in the local schools. The only decent private schools were in Cincinnati and almost all of them were, God forbid, Catholic.

They were both very intelligent but they were mentally slow in many ways. Their minds wondered easily and they had a very hard time controlling their emotions. I had developed a unique way of teaching them in short periods of time taking many breaks for stretching and playing.

They loved to be around other children but they had no friends except for each other. They desperately needed to be around other kids who were around the same age.

I decided that I would take in, and take care of up to five additional children who were mildly mentally retarded.

I would agree to care for and teach these children for free and their parents could visit or take the children anytime they wished.

I placed ads in various papers from Dayton to Lancaster to Chillicothe. I quickly located two girls and three boys. I hired Margie to help me several days a week with bathing and any potential medical needs. This was an incredible amount of work and I learned rapidly that caring for these kids was a 24/7 job with no time for art and no time for myself, but I was very satisfied and the kids were a joy to be around.

In the first few weeks of having all of the kids, I had to fence in the pond so no one would drown, and lock up the barns so that no one would hurt themselves.

My methods of getting the children to learn and retain information seemed to be very effective.

First we started on social skills, such as introductions and basic courtesies when greeting.

Whenever you were introduced to someone you would say, "Hello or how do you do, my name is - *blank* - and I am very pleased to make your acquaintance."

Or if you are introduced to someone you already know, it is polite to tell the introducing third party that you have already been acquainted.

Seven mentally deficient children all shaking each other's hands and saying, "How do you do" or "very pleased to make your acquaintance" was so incredibly comical it almost seemed like a *Three Stooges* short!

I would walk outside of the room and listen to them and I would laugh so hard I would occasionally end up crying. I wasn't laughing at the children or because the children were special, I was laughing because it was just so dammed funny.

These kids were so serious and so eager to be like everyone else. I could only imagine what Hollis would think with all of this going on in his house. I am sure his liquor supply would have depleted rapidly.

It was incredibly gratifying to experience the children retaining and utilizing the information they were learning.

They were proud to know things, they craved recognition and they received as much as I could give them. I also taught them to recognize each other's accomplishments and to complement each other.

Next we learned and practiced table manners and skills that included utilizing a proper place setting, what utensils to use, how to set, where to put our hands, etc. This was a tremendous challenge, but in time all of the children had learned the basics. I noticed how much they loved to correct each other for the smallest infractions, but at least it was my assurance they were learning and retaining information.

Finally we learned proper hygiene and hand washing. We also learned basic first aid and what to do if someone passed out, became ill or cut themselves.

We practiced everything for several months. I thought it was now time to test them in public.

OH MY.

Teaching the kids that someone just casually saying hello, didn't mean that each of them should line up, (while arguing who would be first) each requiring a formal introduction and at least a sentence about the weather or some other small talk from their new acquaintance.

Thankfully the first person they *mobbed* was the local director of the funeral parlor. He graciously donated forty five minutes of his day *formally* meeting each of the children who were all extremely eager to utilize their newly learned social skills in public.

After shaking each of the boys' hands repeatedly, his arm temporarily treated as a pump handle, he finally and gratefully broke free from our group.

We then made our way to the restaurant in town. Again the kids would stop people while they were seated and eating, trying to introduce themselves.

If that was not enough, they quickly dispersed throughout the restaurant instructing the local *hillbilly*'s on how to properly set, how to hold their silverware, how to greet their hostess and always to have only one arm in operation unless cutting, serving or buttering.

I spent ten or so minutes rounding them up, getting AND keeping them seated.

A few of the patrons were furious, most were happy, some were laughing hysterically and so was I.

To hear bits and pieces of EXACTLY everything I had taught these children solely directed at the devoid of etiquette locals, (some of whom were cutting meat with their own dirty pocket knife), thrilled me to no end.

It went something like this:

"We must set properly, with a napkin in our laps, hold our spoon with our right hand, place our left hand at our side or across our laps palm down, and NEVER resting on the table, not even during prayer."

We dined. I apologized en masse and we quickly departed.

I learned an important lesson this day, the delicate subtleties of human behavior that I had taken for granted my entire life, were going to be very hard to teach these children. These children lived in an absolute, almost binary world. They were under the mistaken impression that everyone was reasonably friendly and fair and that right was right and wrong was wrong.

Shades of gray, subtle expressions and most innuendo would completely escape the children a great deal of the time. My work was cut out for me. I was so proud and so happy.

One thing that the children understood with absolute certainty was love. They understood that being kind to each other and being kind to other people they did not know was important.

Being kind made them feel good. Holding a friend's hand or my hand made them feel secure.

From the first day with all of the children we said a special prayer every night before bed.

They would all stand in a circle holding hands and say:

"You will love me as I will love you. Together we will be kind and we will be grateful to all. We will give of ourselves and be thankful for the charity of others. Amen."

A Trunk Full of Fun

As it would turn out, many of the items Hollis had left behind became very useful with the kids.

Hollis left us a wonderful radio with an outside aerial that would pick up radio stations in other countries and even conversations between people. We would typically tune to stations from Cincinnati.

A new type of music was emerging that was becoming very popular. I watched all of the kids singing and dancing to a song called "Rocket 88."

Hugh and Ursal were singing, *"You may have heard of jalopies, you heard the noise they make, let me introduce you to my Rocket '88."*

They would sing this repeatedly. They loved it.

The children loved to dress up with all of the old costumes left in the house.

I would allow them to wear whatever they wanted as long as nothing was exposed that shouldn't be.

Hugh and one other boy, Ronnie would dress in the fake German Army uniforms mimicking the actions of German soldiers while acting like they were speaking in German, stiffly marching, clicking their heels and saying *"Heil Shitler"* to each other. It was hilarious.

Hugh and Ursal loved to wear dresses. Ursal decided that he would like to wear women's clothes all of the time. I was concerned about this, but I allowed it. I had always noticed that Ursal seemed slightly effeminate.

I had always suspected that he was a homosexual. It didn't matter and I would continue to show him the love that I always had.

Soon I would allow Hugh to lead all of the children into town daily to get ice cream, wearing makeup, lip stick, dressed in badger coats, raccoon hats, high heels, army boots, wedding gowns, fluffy feather stoles with army uniforms and wigs.

They had so much fun and all of them laughed. It was good to see them enjoying life. For the entire summer Hugh and Ursal would lead all of the children into town and back for daily ice cream.

I mistakenly assumed that with the children being so obviously mentally deficient, they would just naturally be afforded additional considerations when at play or in public. This was a massive error on my behalf. I would pay dearly and I should have known. I should have known that the same group of people who hated me would also hate anything I would have any involvement with.

On one early fall day on the way home from getting ice cream, Ursal who was always at the rear of the pack, was practicing his May West voice and walk.

He was lured down an alley and beaten severely for wearing girl's clothes and acting like a girl.

Well looky here boys, we got us a retard dressin like a girl.

All of the kids watched as Ursal was beaten and kicked until he went limp.

Ursal would die several weeks later, never waking from a coma caused by many blows to the head.

I was in disbelief, I was in shock. I knew from that point forward that my life would never be what I had hoped for. I would never again feel, act or imagine normal. Suicide seemed fair and easy.

I learned that the real killer of Ursal was an uneducated fifteen-year-old boy who had repeatedly stomped on his head and kicked him in the face and neck screaming at him the entire time. During the beating Ursal had tried to shake the boys hand and introduce himself over and over. Instead he was punched in the face and he fell to the ground. He begged the boy to stop, while still trying to properly introduce himself until he was no longer conscious.

I was arrested and the children were all removed from my custody. I was charged with being an unfit parent, promoting and allowing deviant behavior, running an illegal school for the mentally retarded, and a charge of neglect leading to untimely death.

None of the children would be permitted to testify because of their limited mental capacity.

I prayed for the first time in my entire life.

I begged for death.

The Final Trial

In the judge's chambers before opening statements with prosecutor Helmoth and Judge Wadson:

Yer honor, we gonna send this kike a packin back to the filth she came from, sell that "den of inequity" on the hill to the highest bidder and build a new courtroom with air conditionin outta the proceeds!

I hear'd that. Good, that's real good. Let's get this show on the road.

At this the door to the Judge's chamber closed loudly, rattling the large frosted glass window that held his name.

The bailiff seated the court: All rise, the Honorable Michael T. Wadson presiding, this court is now in session.

The Judge broke the gavel and summoned the prosecutor to the bench. Prosecutor you may proceed with the State Vs. Widow Violet Hoffmiller.

Prosecutor: Madam Widow Hoffmiller, are you represented by counsel?

Violet: Does it matter to you that these children are nourished and healthy, does it matter that these children are happy and they have learned to do some things for themselves?

Prosecutor: Madam, please you're disruptin the proceeding…

Violet: You will poison this jury with manipulations and prejudices.

Prosecutor: The only thing we're going to poison these fine people with is the truth. Madam, yer a small step from contempt. Again, are you represented by counsel, yes or no?

Violet: No.

Prosecutor: Please enter that into the court record. Your Honor may I proceed with opening statements?

Judge: Proceed.

Mam, to step back and address the abject ignorance I heard from you just a moment ago; how could being fed and clean matter when one of the adopted children formerly in your care is dead? From what we understand, the boy most likely perished from trying to perpetrate a heinous homosexual act on another young man in an alley.

How could being fed matter when you allowed these pitiful children of limited mental capacities to stroll about our fine community dressed in Jerry uniforms raising their arms like little Nazis while singing Negro songs with all of them being fully white?

Violet: They were just costumes, they were pretending.

Pretending. . . well that's comforting to know mam. Children not knowing the difference, pretending to be dedicated servants to one the most evil men that the world has ever known . . . Fully white children walkin about singin and hummin darky songs . . . I wonder how and where could they have learned such behaviors, Madam?

Most children pretend to be Cowboys and Indians, or the little girls play with dollies and pretend to be their mommy and such. But not the freak show you put on, NOoooo mam. The freak show that you facilitate teaches kids that it's okay, hell it's even all right if you're a girl dressed and parading about as a boy or god forbid vice-versa. It's okay to be talkin like girl and looking like a boy when you's the opposite.

You heard of dubbya dubbya II madam? The WAR? What are we supposed to tell our fine men who are coming home from fighting this evil when two little retards wearin jerry uniforms are doin the Nazi salute to our boys as their steppin off the bus taking their first breath of Highland County air in nearly three years? Some of them deformed, maimed and shell shocked. What do we say? Welcome home to crazy town?

And you bein a Jew to boot, they were fightin to save your precious people madam . . . God's chosen ones.

What will our fine soldiers think of their homeland when the first thing they see while rolling into town is two retarded boys holding hands walking through town with house coats on and ladies hats a wearin lipstick?

Allowin boys in your group a' scoundrels to dress like women wearin face powder and army boots with coon skin hats.

You see Mam . . . this makes no dammed sense to me or the people in this county. That's why you are here madam.

The problem as we see it Madam, is that all of this must make some dammed sense to you.

Madam you are ill, you are sick and you have no business being around children and certainly no business raising them. Let me tell you mam, allow me to publicly inform you, you will NOT be raising any more kids in this county; you will NOT even live in this county.

In court Violet is severely chastised for taking the Williams to court after accusing the family of abuse and running them out of town while a few years later she creates a "freak" factory encouraging deviant and homosexual behavior.

In an agreement with the court, Violet must leave the county and the State of Ohio. The Westland property is ultimately taken over by the county due to delinquent taxes.

The kids desperately cry and so does Violet when they are taken from her. They all scream for her, most of them cannot understand what has happened or why.

Fearing the worst before trial, Violet had secretly started a trust account for each of the children with all of her remaining cash, the largest of which for Hugh.

For the second time in just over a year she is again thrust into complete and irreparable agony.

Violet walked to the bus stop nearly penniless. She has just enough for bus fare to Cincinnati and train fare to Chicago. Having missed the final bus of the day to get to Cincinnati, she sets on an apple crate next to the curb pondering what to do.

While setting and staring off into the distance, the misery of her experience in this dammed state sets in. No one even notices her. Like the rest of Southern Ohio, the hot news is still the missing Sheriff two counties over from a few months back.

After setting there for more than an hour not knowing what she will do, Violet is offered a ride by a very kind young man from Waverly, Ohio. Throwing caution to the wind, she accepts the offer.

This pleasant man from Waverly doesn't appear to have a care in the world.   His 1946 Ford pickup is spotlessly clean. He has to drive to Dayton but offers to take her to Cincinnati afterwards.

This kind fellow offers to buy her dinner at his favorite restaurant in Dayton, Ohio and with stomach growling, Violet graciously accepts. On the nearly three hour journey from Dayton to Cincinnati, Violet falls asleep about two thirds of the way. Her driver drops a carefully folded $50 dollar bill into her purse. She is awakened as they are pulling up to the Union terminal. Violet thanks the man and they part.

As he is pulling away he hollers at her: "Mam, better check your purse."

In his side mirror he watches Violet find the money as he pulls away, she bends down crying with both hands on her legs, watching the truck as it slowly putts out of sight.

Violet catches the first train to Chicago the following morning at 4:10 a.m. As the train rolls through the countryside she looks at all of the farms and thinks of Bernard.

She cries without caring who sees her. She has lost more than she will ever regain. She will stay with her mother, create art, and live as a recluse for the rest of her life, never leaving the comfort and security of Chicago.

Chapter 9, The Sheriff's Wife

Janet Gifford was one of those women who are physically beautiful but blissfully ignorant. While some would call her a *whore*, she certainly was a pretty one, and pretty always gets by in this world, one way or another. Although it seems that some women just dread sex, Janet Gifford was not one of those women.

Sheriff Gifford left before sunup and returned after dark every day of every week, summer or winter, he never saw his wife in the daylight. He never noticed her dissatisfaction with his very presence. To him, her actions were normal and predictable, that was all about to change. Every day the Sheriff walked in and hung his side arm and hat up next to the door, walked to the table and set down for a waiting cup of coffee and any leftover supper in the stove.

But this day was different.

He instead watches out the kitchen window as Leon Robarts runs through his neighbor's back yard, having no idea that Leon had just jumped out of the bedroom window of his own house.

The Sheriff figured that Leon was up to something, but this was nothing new.

In normal fashion Sheriff Charlie Gifford sets down and leans his chair back on two legs to open the oven and remove a plate of whatever had been placed there by his wife Janet. This time the oven was empty.

Just then Janet entered the kitchen and the Sheriff noticed something that he had never noticed before, Janet wasn't wearing any undergarments. To a normal man a luscious silhouette like Janet's would at a minimum temporarily trump any plate of leftovers that may be waiting in the oven, for Sheriff Gifford, this had never been the case.

He was so continually worried about the illegal beer sales and his own insecurities that sexual activity was not possible and hadn't been for years.

Even years earlier when Janet would come to bed nude, smelling of lavender dragging herself across him, he would always turn her away.

On the way into the house on this particular evening the sheriff had noticed a small pile of old gold cigarette butts in their yard and he inquired.

Did you take up tobacco Janet?

Brimming with absolute contempt, Janet smugly replied, there have been cigarette butts in the yard for several years darlin, wanna know why?

A long and confused silence continued from the Sheriff as he sat looking at her with mouth open, dreading what would be next. She was obviously furious.

Well I'll tell you why God dammit, because the same man who likes my tits hanging free likes to smoke those cigarettes, the same man who craves my lavender scented body and delights me from head to toe, fills your perfect God dammed yard with cigarette butts every other day right after he fills me to the brim.

Wanna know what else he likes . . . Do you want to know just how good he feels in me when I let go on him?

In the beginning, I wished it was you, but now I am glad it ain't because Leon is a MAN . . . shaking her head yes. Oh YES, yes he knows me quite well.

I love to let go on Leon, and sometimes I finish off three or four times before I send his drunken ass on its way.

The Sheriff screamed, So, while yer fully nude in the daylight hours, you pleasure Leon with the sex act in my home and in my bed and that's okay? I provide for this family, everything I have I share with you and only you. But you, oh, you share yourself, your body with the dumbest sumbitch possible. Janet my darling, you can't possibly love Leon can you? He's an idiot just a God dammed fool!

It's true Charlie, I don't love him, I really don't . . . but I dammed sure hate you, I hate everything about you. If you stopped breathin right now, I would never even…

Shut up, just SHUT up! God dammit! Desperately sobbing, the Sheriff falls to the floor unable to utter another word. Janet leaves for her sisters in Marietta, Ohio, slamming the door behind her.

Daughter Jenny goes to a friend's house for a few days and then for good.

Sheriff Gifford is devastated and talking to himself out loud as he paces the floor. The distractions of life had blindsided him completely.

"Weeping Jesus, what the hell have I done to deserve this? It's that God dammed alcohol; it's my punishment for the beer. "

In the Sheriff's mind he figured that the beer he helped bootleg had somehow permitted a drunken Leon to molest his wife. Tears turned to hatred and hatred to rage.

Staying up all night cleaning and re-cleaning his gun, he leans back in his chair again and again looking into the empty stove. He lays his head on the table while crying, drifting off to sleep for a few minutes at a time. He thinks of how good it will feel to finally kill Leon and what he will say when he takes him from this life.

The next day he plans to make the usual beer run. This time he stops at the station and asks Leon to join him. While this was highly unusual, being the credulous idiot that Leon was, he took it as a great compliment.

Well Sheriff I am just surprised . . . REAL suprised. I am pleased to go with ya. Hell we can even hit a few joints along the river on the way back.

Nodding with absolute hatred, the sheriff doesn't utter a word.

The ride to outside of McGaw, Ohio was a quiet one. After twenty minutes of just the sounds from the road, Leon is as fidgety as five year old at a candy counter.

Let's run with the Siren on Sheriff?

Well why not Leon, after all were jist on our way to pick up a trunk load of illegal beer and smokes you god dammed idiot, hell we ain't even in Pike County.

Then Leon asks if the can listen to the radio, the Sheriff glares at him, shakes his head and says nothing.

Finally they arrive at the Ohio Stone & Rock Co. They drive back a long-dirt and gravel lane to a gate where a heavily armed man stood inside a check-in shack next to a dysfunctional truck scale.

With a puzzled look Leon just can't stand it.

Sheriff why are we at this old quarry?

It's not a workin quarry . . . it's a front ya moron.

Well how in the hell would I know?

You would know cause I jist told ya dumbshit. Now zip that dammed yap till we get the hell out of here.

Leon grunts, quickly crossing his drunken arms acting as if his feelings are hurt.

Driving almost a half a mile back they get to the warehouse right next to the river.

Four different gravel trucks rolled in and out five days a week. The owner would load and unload trucks and have his men drive the trucks hell west and wide. No one ever noticed they had never actually delivered anything. Everything looked legitimate but not one pebble was ever sold to anyone.

The Sheriff and Leon are hurried into and through a large building where they remained in the car. Hand trucks and carts were rolling everywhere. There must have been five thousand pallets of beer and another three thousand pallets of cigarettes.

The Sheriff handed a man a big wad of money and the key to the trunk. The trunk was loaded down with beer and cigarettes.

Leon was amazed, and the questions began.

So Sheriff, why are all these here workers chinks?

Because just like you Leon, they can't speak a god dammed lick o' clear English, so they dammed sure ain't gonna squeal. Besides, they don't understand their breakin the law.

Well hell, they's re-labelin beer Sheriff, that's got to be illegal.

I know that God dammit, even you know that. But these chinks here are straight off the boat. Jeeesus Christ Leon, everything about the bootleggin business is illegal, including hauling suds in the back of my dammed cruiser, . . . just shut the hell up.

Leon smiled from ear to ear; he had never imagined an operation like this.

The cigarettes were transported across the river from a tobacco plant in Maysville, Kentucky. They were actually unmarked Grade B bulk packaged for export then stamped and re-packaged in counterfeit Old Gold packs at the warehouse.

The beer was transported down the Ohio River from Pennsylvania. The bottles were soaked in a solution of warm vinegar water to get the labels off. The beer was then relabeled as a higher quality brew from Cincinnati. The re-branded Pilsner was actually just multiple brands of skunky Pennsylvania piss water. About twenty Chinese immigrants repacked the cigarettes and re-labeled the beer. They would work all day and half the night for a dollar.

In a bone dry county the always ice cold beer and cheap cigarettes sold like a Gilded King James at a tent revival.

Finally they left.

Leon was mesmerized by the entire operation and would not shut up. The sheriff had about all he could take and he reminded Leon that they were not friends.

On the way back the Sheriff stopped the car on his favorite road in the county. It was the high point of the area and the nearly hidden narrow pull-off overlooked the valley. The Sheriff knew every inch of this valley and he loved it. Trumpet vines were in bloom everywhere and the smell of late summer was in the air. So many locusts were going off that it sounded like a symphony.

Without a word spoken, they just sat there. At least ten minutes passed by seeming like a few hours. Leon finally asks the Sheriff what the problem is, and if he can have a beer.

With tears running down his cheeks and his voice crackling and sobbing he responds, Leon I know you have been gettin on with my wife Janet for some time now . . . and Janet . . . well

. . . . . . She is a sick woman, she is a real sick woman and I want you to leave her alone. Fact is, you ain't gonna have another chance to molest her or anyone else.

The Sherriff quickly pulled his Colt 45 from under the seat and jammed it in Leon's face.

Leon wasn't surprised. Well if you're gonna shoot me then I wished I had two dicks so I coulda laid into Janet with both of um. Maybe we could trade out for a while. I could take up with her and you could stay at the trailer. You know Sheriff, you ain't always speakin the truth. Just because Janet and I have a special fondness for each other don't mean you have the high ground…

Leon, everything I do is for my family. I may not always be telling the truth, but you ain't never laced its boots.

At this, the Sheriff presses the gun dammed near through Leons jaw and Leon nervously dares the Sheriff to pull the trigger.

Go ahead and shoot me, shoot me God dammit you aren't going to make anything worse for me, it's true . . . it's true, you can take Leon right on out of Pike County, but you ain't takin the nasty outta Janet! Ain't nobody takin'na nasty from that girl . . . NOoo sir.

Sheriff you wern't using that pussy, you couldn't have been, I couldn't see it going to waste.

Then like a 10 watt bulb had lit, Leon pauses and with a long drunken smirk he starts to talk and hold back a nervous giggle, breathing through his fingers with his hand pressed tightly against his mouth.

Sheriff before you go and shoot me I think you should know that poor old sick, sick Janet will miss me the most I would imagine, at least recallin all of the nasty talkin she does when she lets go . . . . . . oh and the screamin she does, and her big ole titties a flyin around, well shit son, she is just a nasty girl. Why she wants all I can give er and let me tell ya ole Leon's a given her plenty to work with.

Then Leon pauses . . . but . . . uh . . . I'm a guessin that ya've never seen her all that worked up...?

Picturing all of what Leon was saying was more than the Sheriff could handle. He completely disintegrated.

Leon . . . . . . you are a piece of shit, just an ignorant piece of shit and I hate your God dammed worthless guts. You're a short time away from settin in satan's lap, I'll be waitin for ya.

Quickly and without warning, the Sheriff turned the gun on himself pushed it tight against his temple and pulled the trigger. It was the first time he had ever discharged his side arm while wearing his badge.

The shot sounded like a cannon.

Leon was shocked; he kept feeling his own head every few seconds. He was blinded by blood and totally deaf. He could only hear his heart racing in his head. The car was full of smoke from the gun mixed with fine blood mist. Completely stunned, maybe for the first time ever, Leon realizes that he hasn't been shot as his hearing starts to return.

Half of the Sheriff's head was blown off and Leon is looking at the Sheriff's brains, his body was thrashing violently and blood was slung everywhere.

The Sheriffs body came to rest in Leon's lap, his mouth still moving like a fish out of water as he is trying to speak, but only blood comes out. For a short time Leon is suddenly more sober than he has ever been in his life.

He vomits all over the corpse, trying to push the body aside as he squirms out of the car.

For nearly two hours he walks back and forth, wringing his hands and talking to himself.

Goddam . . . whatta mess . . . what a God dammed mess. Sheriff's a God dammed mess.

Every few minutes he would stop and look in the car hoping he would somehow see something different, wishing the whole thing never happened.

But the carnage tells the story, and that story is: a dead Sheriff, a car full of blood, illegal out of state counterfeit cigarettes, counterfeit beer, and a worthless woman beating drunk who screwed the now deceased sheriff's wife every chance he got.

Instinctively, Leon popped the trunk, chugged three beers and took off with four more stuffed in his jacket pockets. He runs through field after field, only slowing down to chug another beer or toss the empty.

Finally making his way to the station, he screams for Birch. He is covered in mud, burrs, puke, and blood.

Uncle, UNCLE, Uncle, we've got to set down and talk, we got to talk now.

Birch sees the bloody mess all over Leon and quickly asks, what in the hell have you done? Where is the Sheriff?

Well Uncle here is the thang . . .

What thing? What is going on here you God dammed idiot? Where is the Sheriff?

WELL . . . now . . . he's dead.

DEAD! How is he dead? Where is he dead? You dumbass, did you kill him?

No, Uncle . . . well . . . . . . he accidently shot he'self in the head.

Whatttt! Jesus Christ O'mighty . . . you stupid bastard, I should have let you stay at the boy's farm. Where is the Sheriff?

Up on Spruce Ridge road, at the narrow pull-off.

Birch and Leon hop in Birch's wrecker and go back to the Sheriff's car. Birch cannot believe the carnage, Christ Leon what in the hell did you do?

Nothing.

Nothing? Nothing? Then what is this you god dammed moron, what in the hell is this Leon, this ain't nothing. Why is the top of the Sheriffs head blown clean off? No, this ain't nothing Leon, this is a BIG GOD dammed mess.

Leon tells Birch the whole long depressing story, the whole ritual with Janet, everything.

As Leon goes on and on, Birch gazes out over the valley and Leon's words sound like a barely turned up radio late at night.

The reality of this situation is becoming very clear and that is whether Leon killed the Sheriff or the Sheriff killed himself, it isn't going to matter. No one will believe the story no matter who tells it, in no way can this situation be cleaned up at least not cleaned up enough for anyone to make any sense of it. This is the end, the whole dammed thing . . . the beer, the smokes, the repair racket, *all of it*.

Leon goes on and on, over and over again with each new version presenting a new drunken twist.

Birch is a million miles away even with the carnage before him. Birch thinks about being a young man, he thinks about how good Leona would smell and how pretty she was, he remembers wearing some smell'um himself and going out to dinner at a table service restaurant and then some dancing.

He remembers when the self-imposed complexities of life had not yet closed in on him. He remembers slowly dancing with Leona and how her beautiful soft neck felt when he would kiss her.

He questions where those times went and he then looks in the rearview mirror at the unkempt tattered remains of the man once kissing that beautiful woman's neck, and he groans in discontent. Like a lightning bolt, he realizes that only the present is real, it's the only thing that ever is. The past might as well be make believe, because you can't get to it, you can't have it back no matter how much beggin you do. It seems the past is only there to remind you of where you are now, and sometimes *now* ain't too dammed pretty.

Finally after looking out over the valley and listening to a rambling drunk of a nephew for far too long, Birch realizes what must happen.

Leon, we've got to bury this awful mess.

The car and all?

Yes dumbass the car and all. First go get me some rags from the wrecker, and then start cleaning the blood off the windows. Move the Sheriff to the back seat and cover him with a blanket from his trunk.

Leon wrestles the Sheriff's body into the back seat right next to him.

Birch reaches in through the window and asks Leon to hand up the Sheriff's gun.

As Leon sets in the back of the cruiser with the corpse in his lap, Leon hands Birch the Sheriff's still cocked .45.

Birch looks at Leon and sees the little cross eyed boy with pissed pants that he raised nearly all of his life setting in the back seat of the cruiser with the Sheriff. Almost twenty five years flash through his mind.

Birch slowly closes his eyes and blasts that little boy in the top of the head while Leon looks up at him not saying a word. Birch watches Leon slump over on the Sheriff's body, and for the first time since his wife left him, he cries so hard that he can't catch his breath, he clutches his chest and pains shoot down his arms.

He falls to the ground and gets up walking back and forth, looking in the cruiser over and over. Birch wails, he cannot stop crying and he talks to himself out loud while holding on to the back door window, knees against the car, just staring at the carnage.

Weepin' Jesus, what have I done to deserve this, my only friend and my only kin folk, one killed the other and I kilt the one left. He thinks back about killing *Daddy* Ross Setzer when he was a boy.

Birch throws the gun in the back with Leon and the Sheriff and tows the car to a 50 acre piece of ground that he owns behind Leon's old trailer. Pulling back the lane, he hits the front of Leon's trailer, ripping a big chunk of the siding off. The wheels of his wrecker flatten the trailer emblem in to the mud.

Birch fires up his Link-Belt Speeder and rapidly digs a huge hole in the center of a thicket. He buries the car with the bodies of his only friend and his only known relative. He never remembers the beer or cigarettes in the trunk. Birch figures that the four feet of sandy loam on top of the car in the pit he dug will be enough.

By 3 a.m. Birch finally lays down, he cannot believe this day, he could have never imagined what had taken place, but it did. He dreads sun-up and has no idea how he will put this into perspective. He thinks about what a good friend the Sheriff actually was and how much he enjoyed their conversations. He thinks about Leon and how funny he was as a little boy, he remembers that cross eyed little boy riding on a board nailed to skates.

He thinks of killing himself, but he quickly drifts off thinking about Leona.

In a moment of clarity perhaps brought on by the emotional trauma of the day Birch all of a sudden remembers something that he had never thought of since the day Leona had left him. It was his beautiful Leona setting on the side of their bed with her hand on his cheek saying *"I love you Birch, but I have to go. This ain't the life I wanted."*

-Fade to gray-

At 6:45 a.m. one of Birch's everyday customers, Mr. Parnell Washburn is at his door. Normally he would just walk on in. On this morning the door was still locked.

Knock knock knock, Birch, ya up? . . . I'm needin a beer . . . (oh, sorry I meant a quart of oil in a bag) . . . A long pause . . . . . .

Well God dammed, this ain't normal 'tall. Knock knock knock, Birch, ya up? I'm bringin you business man, I needs a beer . . . knock knock, C'mon Birch, well now look at me, I got them bad shakes, lets go…. knock knock . . . I promise I'll be payin ya what I owe in total next week, swear on my mother's grave….knock knock.

Birch . . . BIRCH!

Unknown to Mr. Washburn, Birch will not be answering the door, this day or any day. The pains he had been having in his shoulder were the result of large clog in his circulatory system. He had a massive heart attack in his sleep and died at 4:01 a.m.

As kids make their way out to play and people go about their business, the beautiful Saturday morning sun rises over the station like nothing could possibly be wrong.

What no one will ever know is that three men had stopped living on the same day in a small town, all of them dying for completely different reasons that no longer mattered. Truth is that life killed them all, despite a few pulls of the trigger. Some men die when their supposed to and others die when they have no other choice. But dead is dead, only the living complain.

The town is in a complete uproar, Birch Robarts is found dead, the Sheriff has up and vanished car and all. No one even notices that Leon Robarts is missing.

Rumors of all shapes and sizes would rage on for years. Answers would never be provided at a time when they would have mattered.

A silent curse was about to be unleashed. No one could begin to imagine it.

Chapter 10, Mr. Russ Robarts

A month after his father died; the daily bus from Cincinnati drops off Birch's unknown son Russ in the middle of Chillicothe, Ohio. He thumbed a ride to Waverly.

Russ was dammed near penniless. His mother Leona had died a year earlier from kidney failure. His bankrupt stepfather had always known that Russ wasn't his child. He told Russ where his Mother was from and where he might find his real Father. Leona had kept the family in receivership nearly all of their life.

Everyone in the area is talking about what happened and Russ found Birch's place locked up tight with every window boarded up. Extremely depressed, he sets in the tall weeds at the edge of town with his last candle pondering what to do.

Russ had slept in the rough for several days. He hadn't had more to eat than a dozen summer apples in nearly two days and he was running out of broad leafed plants at his favorite spot to shit in the woods. As hungry as he was, another apple probably wouldn't make it to his stomach, and if it did make it, it was going to make a dammed fast exit out the other end.

Figuring he has nothing to lose, he breaks into the station that night and pokes through his father's things. He wants something, anything that was his fathers or his mothers. He sees all of the accumulated parts, candy, bags, papers and calendars. This place is amazing. The smells, and the massive accumulations of items that made no sense whatsoever, every stack was the same, with the oldest of whatever it was being at the bottom of a stack and the newest at the top.

Russ finds a picture of a young Birch Robarts, the resemblance was unquestionable, and Birch had to have been his father. He tries to put his unknown Father's life into perspective.

He then finds the only picture of his Mother and Father that he has ever seen, he breaks down and wonders why his life ended up the way that it had, completely apart from who he should have grown up with.

His mother had decided that protecting a lie would forever be more important than a boy knowing his real father. As much as it bothered him, it didn't matter as hunger pains were rapidly undermining the scorn of the moment.

Nearly starving to death, he cooks four eggs in the only skillet he can find, eating with the only fork available. Setting his parents picture up on the table and leaning it against a chair, Russ looks at his mom and dad with questions that will never be answered. Unknown to him, he eats the same thing his father would have eaten with the same fork out of the same skillet. When he finishes, he sticks the heavy old bent up fork in his shirt pocket.

Nothing was new, everything was old. He could not imagine the life his Father must have lived.

Russ continues the hunt. Finding a musty cooler room full of warm beer and cigarettes, he figures out that his father was a bootlegger among other things.

Russ realizes that his father must have had a safe, because He can't find any official paper bearing his father's name.

Birch lived a life of cash only. He never had a social security number. For his entire life the federal government had somehow overlooked Birch Robarts and he had dammed sure overlooked them.

Russ despises the fact the he has to secretly hurry through the only evidence of his real family that he has ever seen. For now, having nothing but the clothes on his back must trump figuring out his family tree.

He had never seen so many car parts and manuals. He searches through his father's belongings like a bloodhound.

Finding an old lard bucket full of quarters he stuffs his pockets to the breaking point. Smiling from ear to ear, he feels like he has robbed a bank. However, his luck was about to change. Ten minutes or so later he finds a car key on a chain with a small locket that contained a picture of his Mother in Birch's overall pocket.

Russ opens the trunk to the only car in the yard that the key would fit and nearly passes out. He finds all of Birch's money in the trunk of one special car in the wrecking yard.

The key chain and the locket are placed in the same pocket with the fork.

The trunk contains hundreds of jars full of cash - all half buried and resting in a bed of cedar sawdust. Russ empties his overstuffed pockets of quarters and quickly empties every Mason jar of cash, while quietly and neatly placing all of the jars on Birch's back porch.

Almost reluctantly, he takes the money, all in all over $100,000 in cash. Russ sneaks out of the wrecking yard with all of the cash and the only picture he has ever seen of his parents together in a large canvas draw-bag.

Unknown to Russ, the only two people who would have ever known that Birch would have had a dollar to his name were dead.

A month later, Birch's estate goes to public auction.

Russ watches at a distance with an appreciative smile as his father's estate is sold. All in all the estate sells for $6,700.

Being in the right place at the right time, would never again feel so good. At the estate sale the man who buys the car with a trunk full of cedar sawdust will never know how close he came.

$100,000 was just about a shitload of money in the early 1950s. As tempted as he was to buy dammed near everything in sight, Russ knows that he must keep his act together. He knows that he must buy only what he needs and maybe a little of what he wants over time.

His stepfather did nothing but bitch, his Mother did nothing but spend and his Father obviously did nothing but save. Russ would have to find a comfortable spot right on up the center. This was the gift of a lifetime and he wasn't about to let it slip away because of ignorance. A moderate room by the week in Chillicothe would have to do for a while.

For the first time in many weeks, Russ was thrilled when he hopped up in a freshly whisked out barber's chair for a hot lather shave and a haircut.

The loud click and warm buzz of the shears had never felt so good. Hot towels and a healthy sprinkling of lavender water and powder finished things up.

A burley looking thing may have walked in, but a proud clean cut man walked out. Some new matching Dickie drawers and shirts, and a new pair of boots would complete the transformation.

Confidence restored, he decides to buy a second hand 1946 ford truck in Chillicothe. The truck had less than one thousand miles on it. Russ had never owned or even imagined owning a car or truck in his life.

Several months later, Russ buys a nice little two bedroom house five miles outside of Waverly, Ohio for $2,850 on three and one half acres of ground. It was move-in ready. There was a pump sink in the kitchen and an outhouse with an electric heater. In Russ's eyes, it was a mansion beyond compare.

Lying on the ground behind his new house with his head resting on a round cast iron cistern lid, Russ cries while he smiles looking up at the sky. Going from dammed near nothing to dam near everything in a few weeks' time is one hell of a rollercoaster ride. He thinks of shitting in the woods a month earlier and how nice his outhouse is with a reading lamp and an electric heater, walls and a roof.

Always worried, Russ rightly figures that no one knows him, and he sure doesn't know anyone, so what the hell, a man has to live. Only the passing of time will ease his mind.

He slowly furnishes the little house with second hand items from local auctions. No one asks questions at auctions, you just hand over the cash and load your goods.

Driving for three and a half days round trip to Pittsburg, PA, Russ buys a safe so that he can secretly store the remaining money. He sleeps in his truck on the way there and back, keeping the safe tarped over and chained to the bed of his truck.

Ultimately he concretes the safe into a wall of the cellar. The work takes over two weeks to complete. He nearly breaks an arm while trying to lower the safe into his basement while using a rigged up block and tackle pulley system.

For many weeks now Russ has acted like he would go to work, knowing that any young man driving a newer truck and living around Waverly would have a job.

Every morning at 6:45 a.m. on the dot he would head to his truck with an empty lunch pail, . . . it may have had a hundred or so dollars in it, but no food.

He had a jug of water and an Atlas on the seat, a roll of toilet paper on the dash, two full cans of gas and two spare tires safely roped down and tarped over in the bed of the truck. He would wave to any neighbors he would see and head down the road.

Russ would drive all over the place, only stopping for gas or a meal.

He would sing and sometimes cry, but most of the time he just smiled while cautiously navigating the countryside to destinations only discovered upon arrival. A more grateful man could not be found.

Russ grew up in a rough part of Cincinnati and all of his life he either walked or took the trolley everywhere he had ever been. He could have never imagined owning a car or truck or most of all a home, deed and title in hand.

He drove to Hamilton, Middletown, Dayton and Springfield and every place in between, always avoiding Cincinnati.

Russ would eat at roadside food stands or any place with counter service. He had never eaten at a set down restaurant with table service.

No one knew him and this was the biggest adventure of his life. His favorite place to eat was Kuntz's Café on the northern edge of Dayton, Ohio on Troy Street. He would drive to Kuntz's Café at least once a week.

Russ didn't even have a drivers permit, but in truth about half of the people driving around at the time didn't either. At that time even seeing a kid drive a farm truck was no big deal. If you could reach the pedals, see over the dash and turn the wheel, you could drive. Of course any city driving required good brakes and your full attention.

Russ would pick up hitchhikers, and ask them where they were going. If it was anywhere within a fifty or so mile radius of where they were presently at, he would lie and say he was heading in that general direction.

He would then take his passenger to their destination. Many times on the way he would feed the lucky travelers enroute, stick a ten dollar bill in their pockets and send them on their way.

The most unforgettable ride Russ would ever give to anyone was a lady by the name of Violet Hoffmiller. He would never forget her.

Blonde hair and dark eyes, a fine looking woman, and so dammed sad that you would think she was dying. Russ pulled up to see her crying and setting on an apple crate with her suitcase at the edge of Hillsboro.

The woman was just beside herself, she looked like she had been to hell and back. She needed a ride to Cincinnati to catch a train to Chicago. She was going home to live with her mother. It would be the only time Russ would ever break his own rule about returning to Cincinnati. She told Russ that her husband had died and about some of her time in Hillsboro, she was devastated. Russ wanted desperately to tell her his own story but he reluctantly kept it to himself.

Her story made Russ think even more about blending in and not drawing any attention to himself.

Many years later while talking to an unusual man while visiting his grandson David in Athens, Russ would come to understand just who Violet Hoffmiller was.

After several months of touring Ohio and parts of Northern Kentucky, Russ reluctantly knows that he must actually work. After many weeks of begging for a job and showing up at jobsites while sometimes working for free until discovered, the State of Ohio finally hires him.

Ultimately he meets a beautiful young lady at the Pike County Fair.

He falls head over heels in love with a young lady by the name of Jenny Gifford. They marry and have one child, a little girl named Lindsey.

Many years after they are married he tells Jenny who his real father is and she is shocked, but happy to finally know. She now knows who is in the old picture that Russ has kept hanging in a special closet for years. She encourages Russ to hang the picture in the living room, right next to a picture of her father, Sheriff Charlie Gifford. The old friends were again reunited, side by side looking over a family neither of them could have ever dreamed of sharing.

For nearly fifteen years, Russ deposits almost all of his paycheck into a savings account, drawing down the cash from his safe in the cellar to live on. He will pray to his father every day for the rest of his life, thanking him sincerely for the gift that he had no idea he left, for a son he would never meet.

For every meal he will ever eat, Russ will use his Father's heavy old silver fork that he had stuck in his pocket after finishing the first and only meal he would ever eat in his mother and father's home.

A meal they watched him eat with their picture standing on the table leaning against a chair right next to him.

Chapter 11, June 1981 - Waverly, Ohio

"The twists and turns of this life cannot be relied on or
disregarded; the past ball up and unwinds
for generations, sometimes manifesting itself in ways
that are unimaginable to the reasonably sane mind."

Walt Jenkins had just removed the sold sign from the front yard of his latest sale and placed it in his trunk. As he walked to the house to greet his young clients; Kit and Lindsey Peterson, he hears muted angry voices between his steps in the freshly graveled lane.

As he gets closer, he realizes they are having a major argument before they had even moved in to their new house. He cautiously listened at the edge of the garage but did not fully understand what he was hearing on the other side of the wall.

Kit screamed, well I think the little shit is hallucinating or something, just why in the fuck would a room move?

Lindsey responded, uh huh . . . hallucinating. . . Jesus Kit, it's all black or white in your world. I can't believe I even married you, I just can't believe it.

Well get a lawyer God dammit, I am sure yer daddy will pay for it.

Well why not, Daddy pays for everything else, everything other than for yer stinkin pot.

After standing there and briefly listening to all of this, Walt with eyes closed mumbles "oh God" to himself and now knocks loudly so he can get this over with.

Lindsey opens the door and they all stare at each other in silence for a few seconds. A smile could not be found or traded.

Well hello folks, I u-h . . .I just pulled up . . . I hope you will enjoy your new home Mr. and Mrs. Peterson, it has been a pleasure serving you and I would like to welcome you to the community.

You have purchased a nice home and a beautiful piece of ground here folks; it will only appreciate over time. Say hello to your Dad for me Lindsey.

At this, Walt handed them the spare keys, patted their son David on the head and left as fast as he could shuffle down the lane.

Peculiar couldn't begin to describe Kit and Lindsey's son David. He had wanted to know if each of the rooms in their new house would always be in the same place. Lindsey tried very hard to understand just what David actually wanted to know or was trying to figure out.

As it turned out, David wanted to know this because he was afraid of getting lost and not being able to find his way around the new place. Why David would think like this was perplexing. But from the very beginning Lindsey had learned to ask herself why David would not think something.

Kit was just mad as hell. *I'm tellin ya Linds, that boy would get lost in the shithouse!*

Kit and Lindsey Peterson just purchased their first home. They had lived with Lindsey's parents for a few years and rented for three more.

Kit grew up in West Virginia and met Lindsey or "Linds" as he calls her at an outdoor concert in 1976, The Mosquito Dam Jam.

They hit it off real good. So good in fact that a month after they met Kit received a nice letter and a card informing him that he was going to be a father.

Up to this point, Kit could count his victories in life on one hand and it was becoming increasingly hard for him to stay on the sunny side. He will always remember meeting Lindsey's dad Russ, it wasn't a pleasant introduction, in fact it couldn't have went much worse.

My daughter is with child because of what you did.

Just because of me?

That's right.

I see, I see. Then yer accusin me of forcin sumthin right?

I'm not sure, but I do think she was talked into sumthin' and got caught up in the moment.

Well, let me ask ya Mr. Robarts, are ya sure it was our moment she got caught up in that resulted in her present condition?

You smartass sumbitch, I oughtta cut yer dick off.

If yer man enough to try, I am dammed sure man enough to stop ya. Look man, no seed ever sprouts without a fertile field fer plantin. If you were in my spot, what would you be thinkin?

Russ was welling up, his eyes watering.

With a shakey voice he responds, I ain't in yer spot boy, you are . . . Just talk with Lindsey God dammit, I don't want a bastard grandbaby. My little girl is pregnant and it's a killin me, do you get that boy, my hearts broke in the worst way it ever could be. So I'll put this right back to ya and leave it with ya, if you were in my spot, what would you be thinkin?

Kit and Lindsey were married two weeks later, baby on the way. Their relationship had been strained from the start.

By the time David was fourteen months old he was talking in full sentences. By the time he was three years old he was already scaring the hell out of everyone, drawing unusual pictures and saying unusual things. And now at five, the things he would ask were beyond worrisome, things no kid should be thinking about.

Times were tough in the Buckeye state and work was scarce everywhere, but in Southern Ohio you had to know someone to get even a minimum wage job.

The nation was in a rough transition, politicians squarely blaming each other every morning with the news camera rolling, the blamed and the blamers all cozied up and toasting each other with one hundred year old bottles of scotch, while sharing high dollar hookers later that evening. For all of the on camera squabbles about America's declining morality, it seems these *chappys* could easily agree on which hooker was going to be in their room each night and who was going to pay the bill for it.

Lots of TV promises made, and lots of TV reasons why they were never kept. Kit privately wondered how much shittier things could get. The *peanut farmer* was out and the *actor in chief* was in. For a short time, gas had soared from forty eight cents to a buck thirty five a gallon, many of their friends were unemployed, things were not easy, in fact, things just plain sucked.

Lindsey's father had given Kit and Lindsey half of the purchase price for the house and land as silent insurance that they would remain in the area with his grandson.

In turn, Kit had also agreed to help his father-in-law farm the thirty plus acres of tillable ground starting in the spring.

Kit did not like any part of this arrangement, but beggars can't be choosers and as painful as it was, he dammed well knew which of the two he was.

Kit found the garage door clicker lying on the counter in the kitchen. He hit the button and pulled his orange and white 1970 Chevy truck into the empty garage, opened both doors, kicked his feet up and fired up a big joint. He blew huge smoke rings on exhale and the garage reeked of marijuana.

Bad Company was playing in his cassette deck . . .

His son stared at him from the entryway to the house the entire time and Kit stared back at him without expression.

A half hour had passed and Lindsey is quite pissed. With her hand on one hip and a box on her opposite shoulder, she goes off:

That's just great Kit, sooo responsible, our new house with a million things to do and you are getting stoned and stinking up the garage with that shit while David watches, what a great father.

She continued, I mean what are you going to tell him that you're doing?

Not a fuckin thing Linds, he can see what I'm doing. I ain't ashamed of anything I do. Kit turned his stereo up even louder.

With David still watching, Kit drops his head, turns his back and rubs his neck, then quickly pulls *the bird* out from his collar as she walks away. Unknown to Kit, David mocks him perfectly.

That's real good Kit, real good. I get flipped off for bustin my ass here while you set on yours.

C'mon . . . I'm just fuckin around. You know, I didn't sign up for this boss me every wakin' minute, shit Linds.

Somebody has to boss you if anything will get done.

Goddamn woman, we got all weekend to unpack. Don't you ever fuckin relax? Hit this joint, it's that new shit my cousin's growing: "The weed with no seed."

Uh, I don't think so. I hate that shit and you know it.

You know Linds, the way I see it is that we're dammed near dirt poor and we ended up with a weird as fuck red head of a kid, so takin the edge off is good thing.

It's illegal Kit. It's against the law.

So's speedin, but we both do it every place we go.

That's different.

Bullshit, breakin the law is breakin the law. Speedin will kill ya, specially in this state . . . a little weed ain't gonna hurt ya.

Whatever stoner, start unpackin these boxes.

Oh, well, right away . . . right away . . . Colonel Klink, heil. At this a squinty eyed Kit came to attention, clicked his heels and got to work.

Even from the old crow's viewpoint circling high above the house, the strain inside that young marriage was growing.

Lindsey's father got Kit a job working for the state in highway maintenance, or as Kit said, *"A unionized trash picker."*

Kit had dropped out of school but was slowly studying to get his GED, very slowly.

Kit was a thin man, almost too thin. Three double cheeseburgers at a time wouldn't put an ounce on him. He had sky blue eyes, long medium brown hair and a pleasant smile. While shaving was always optional, a daily intake of weed was not.

Pot seemed to iron out the wrinkles. A good buzz everyday would help him keep things in perspective. Prince, West Virginia seemed like a million miles away.

Lindsey was an average girl with an above average sense of her place in the world. She never wore make up and had never even wore lipstick in her life.

The only thing you would find in Lindsey's purse is a pack of peppermint gum and a tube of Chap-stick. Her hair was mostly blonde in the summer and mostly light brown the rest of the time. Some would say she was a little mousey, while others would say that she gets prettier the longer you know her.

She grew up in Waverly, Ohio and her father worked for the State of Ohio roads department as a manager. Lindsey finished high school and was taking classes for an associate degree in accounting.

The youngest member of the Peterson family was David. David was a red-head just like his grandfather Russ, with silver dollar freckles.

Red headed people are dammed near a different species. While there opinions and lifestyles may be at extremes, so is everything else about them.

It was like any other day for David Peterson, he was five, school didn't start until September and the fifty acres his family now owned just outside of Waverly, Ohio was a good place to be.

A little creek, and rolling hills should be enough to keep any boy happy, but *happy* usually didn't apply to David Peterson. While he would appear content, happy would seem a far stretch.

Recently David had started to ask his mother about death and what it meant to die. This troubled her, but all kids ultimately ask about things like this so she was temporarily comforted by that fact.

She had tried to explain to David that our bodies quit working at some point in our life and that we just cease to exist.

She wasn't going to attempt the religious aspect of anything with him, she knew that would result in never ending barrage of questions.

What was distressing was when she asked David what he thought about death. David basically explained the best he could that he thought when you died it was like walking from one room into the other without wanting to or being able to return to the room you came from. Lindsey was startled by this. Kit completely despised the subject and thought something was wrong with his son. To David the dead didn't ever really go away, they were somewhere.

Asking David questions always meant that you had to emotionally prepare yourself for whatever he might say in response. His thoughts and rationales were often just as hard to dispute as they were to support.

Then there was the puppy incident.

Kit and Lindsey found a black lab puppy for David, they named him Charcoal. The puppy ended up dead the very next day.

Kit saw David pulling the dead puppy around by his collar as if nothing at all was wrong. He was beyond pissed off.

Jeeeesus Christ David, what did you do to the puppy?

Nothing, he is so pretty for me, she still loves me.

He ain't lovin anybody now Goddammit, he's deader than a fuckin door nail. What did you do?

David just stood there looking around.

Kit was enraged and he hollered for Lindsey.

Tell your mother what you did David.

David continues to just look around, he turns and starts to walk away, dead puppy in tow.

Kit grabbed him by both shoulders, shaking him while screaming, what in the fuck did you do David?

Lindsey interrupts, We aren't going to find out by beating him Kit!

Well, we aren't going to find out at all Linds, cause the sneaky little shit will make up a big lie and you will buy it, and there we'll be. Fuck it, I'm going to bury the poor thing and you can deal with Damien the dammed puppy slayer.

You know Kit, sometimes things just die. We got him for free…

Bullshit Linds, he killed the poor thing. That puppy didn't just die and you dammed well know it . . . Fuckin weird ass kid . . . Free don't mean you get to kill somethin Linds. My old man woulda beat me half to death for somethin like this.

Yes, and what would that do Kit? What would hitting David do?

Fuck it then, you deal with him. I'm out.

Two afternoons later, Lindsey finds David with the dead puppy again; he had unearthed the puppy as if nothing was wrong.

Lindsey is upset, but she chalks it up to childhood curiosity. She also just figures that David misses the puppy, he had no other playmates.

David, I know you miss puppy, but we have to leave him buried honey, he is dead. We will get a new puppy soon.

But mommy I want this one. He's puppy does just what I tell it to do, but it stinks, I still want it but it stinks.

Quite worried, Lindsey buries the puppy at her parents' house, never mentioning it to Kit. David was furious and insisted the puppy was his, alive or dead.

David's unusual behavior was taking a toll on his parents, especially Kit.

On many mornings or even in the middle of the night, Kit or Lindsey would wake up only to find David standing at the foot of their bed or right beside them, wide awake, just looking at them, in an empty way, not smiling . . . He would never make a sound. Lindsey always defended his odd behavior.

Kit, he just watches us, he never bothers anyone.

Look, knowing anyone is just watching me while I sleep bothers me.

How could it, you're sleeping?

Well if I roll over and I see him starin straight at me, I sure as hell can't get back to sleep, and you get pissed if I schoo him off.

What do you want him to do Kit?

What do I want him to do? I want him to stay in his dammed room, that's what. At least until I wake up. If you want him to watch you while yer sleepin, that's up to you. I'll sleep in my dammed truck if I have to.

The uncertainty of David's actions caused an endless war.

While she thought it would be good for David to make some friends, Lindsey was already dreading the thought of him starting school. Kit just figured he had the type of boy who would get a daily ass kickin, and that nothing much could be done about it.

Even with his peculiarities David was still a little boy. He hated going to bed and was usually up and ready to play by the time the birds were singing. Summer days in southern Ohio were beautiful.

Each and every day David would slowly disappear over the hill behind the house into the rolling field. A fair portion at one corner of their property was a dense thicket. It would take a month of chainsaw work and bush-hogging just to make a path. David had been warned not to play there until it was cleared out.

Mommy I am going to dig for treasure back in the field.

Okay dear, but please be careful.

Several hours later David returned.

Mommy the man leans back in she's chair to open he's stove, then lays she's head on the table.

David, what are you talking about?

The man in the field.

Is this something from a TV show?

No, he's my friend.

What's your friend's name?

Grampa.

David, grampa lives down the road.

Not my grampa mommy, your grampa.

Confused by this, Lindsey walked to where David had been. She made him stand at the back of the house. There was no one.

This was not the first time Lindsey had heard some version of this from David and she was on high alert.

Perhaps he was actually describing something he had briefly seen on television. Or perhaps it was an imaginary friend. She privately feared this was not the case.

David was hard to get accurate information from. He would often describe just a portion of something. Then, if that wasn't confusing enough, you didn't know if he was relaying information about something a few days ago or if he was talking about something new. Just trying to pin him down on *when* was almost impossible.

As they lay in bed that night, Lindsey tells Kit about what David has been saying.

It is starting to bother me Kit, he has said this to me each day for the last few days. I looked around and I didn't see anybody.

Well maybe the puppy that he **didn't** kill is coming back to haunt us.

After a long pause, Lindsey continues; that's not funny Kit, I'm serious. It's starting to give me the creeps, it bothers me; it bothers me really bad. I don't know how to respond. I mean, what do I say to say to him? He isn't smiling when he tells me about this.

With complete contempt Kit quietly states: Well, I never see David smile much about anything.

Lindsey looks at the ceiling and rolls her eyes.

Kit sighs and grunts for a few seconds, well . . . shit Linds, in the morning talk to him about it again and if you are still upset about it we can watch him for a few days to see if we make some sense of it.

The next morning is quiet, no noise, no cars, no planes, not many birds singing, just the voices of David and his mom can be heard and a slight air noise circulating through the house.

It's almost like the spoken word was staying close that day and not traveling through the air to the ear of the recipient. Instead, your words seemed to curve back to your own ear.

Things were tense, this day was unusual and Lindsey was completely on edge. Her chest was tight; it seemed hard to breathe. She was dreading the conversation with David.

David worried her; the simplest things, odd things, could mesmerize him. Before she asked him to talk, David had entranced himself rolling a truck in circles from the wood floor, to the linoleum entrance, to the area rug. Over and over, the sound of each transition created an odd rhythm.

Once he would start something like this, anything that was rhythmic, he would have to be forced to stop and when he was, it was never pleasant, it was as if something very sacred was being taken from him, something important. Everything he did was synchronized in some way, and had some sort of rhythmic timing.

When David would eat, each bite that he would take had to be equally spaced from the last. He would chew each bite exactly as the last, four times on the left side, four times on the right side, then swallow.

His shoes would have to be exactly the same tightness, tied exactly with the same tension with the loops the same size.

The slightest difference in his actions or his surroundings would cause David great stress. Symmetry was extremely important to him. All of this drove Kit nuts. He could not believe that his son was this weird.

Everything was a ritual with David and all of these rituals insured that David's existence was peaceful and right.

The air noise circulating in the house was now louder, and Lindsey was experiencing extreme anxiety. After putting it off for far too long, she finally asks David about the man.

David, I want to ask you some questions about the man or whoever it is that you see in the field, okay?

Okay mommy.

At this time, David is staring off into some other place and while he was not physically distracted he was certainly mentally distracted. He was just standing there watching the TV, but not really looking at it. His favorite part of The Captain Kangaroo show, Picture Pages was coming on.

"Picture pages picture pages time to get your picture pages, time to get your crayons and your pencils," played quietly in the background . . .

David, are you telling mommy a lie about the man in the field?

With virtually no expression and no eye contact David replies, no mommy, no I 'm not lying. The man leans back in he's chair to open he's stove and then lays he's head on the table and cries, lots of times.

What man, David?

The man in the car mommy.

What man in the car David?

After a very long pause an impatient and very frustrated David rapidly says, the man who holds he's head and cries at he's stove and says sorry all the time and other stuff.

David, you must tell me exactly where this man is, where is this man in the car and in a chair next to his stove?

David responded that he was in the field with the treasure.

Does this man talk to you David?

Not in my ears. After another long pause he says, he won't look to see me.

Lindsey is damned near cringing, she knows there is more to this than what David can accurately describe.

David, what you said to mommy doesn't make any sense. Again Lindsey insists, David how can you see this man if he cannot see you? How do you know he can't see you?

But . . . but . . . mommy, I screamed and he don't even move.

David can you show me this man?

After a long and unusual stare from David, he answers, yes if I can find him.

You have to look for the man David?

Yes, he hides from me.

Lindsey was now even more concerned, David's answers made no sense. But she knew that David wasn't lying. David had never lied about anything before, he had been misunderstood, but he had never really lied.

So the next day David makes his way back through the pasture. Through the Queen Anne's lace and cornflowers he went. The sky was overcast. Suddenly David stops and slowly walks back and forth four or five steps at a time just like he is on a balance beam. His head would turn back and forth in increments like the seconds ticking on a clock. It was quite a spectacle. Without a word spoken, David repeated this ritual over and over for at least 45 minutes.

Kit and Lindsey watched this from several hundred feet away. At times David would hold so perfectly still that he would almost vanish into the landscape.

Finally Kit smirks at Lindsey and mumbles while shaking his head: Just a fuckin waste of time.

They both walked to where David was standing.

After a long stare Kit asks: So . . . David, where is this man?

David points and says that he's hiding.

His mother asks, hiding where David?

Out there in the field mommy.

Well there you go darlin, there ya go, said Kit. Just like I thought, your mystery man is just a made up five-year-old boy's line of shit.

Lindsey interrupts, but Kit, he says this same thing to me almost every day and I don't understand why he would lie about this, this isn't like eating his green beans and *forgetting* about the number of bites he takes. Don't you think we should look around?

Look around for what? Jesus Christ Linds, will you believe any fuckin thing? Is everything the little shit says true? Woman he's five, and half of what he comes up with is just bullshit, you . . . know . . . that. Besides that he can't talk for shit. He always gets his Rs and his he's and she's all fuckin mixed up, only you and I know what the hell he is saying half of the time and sometimes we have to put that to a vote.

I don't think he even knows difference in boys from girls, and we've both tried to tell him.

For a few minutes they all just stand there looking around.

Finally in a very strained voice Kit half leans over and whispers to Lindsey, *we do need to find a man Linds, but he ain't in this field. We need to find a Doctor because this weird ass kid is ill, something is wrong here Linds, now, you've got to see it, he ain't right in the head.*

All hell breaks loose and Lindsey is furious.

Oh is that so Kit, well this "weird kid" is your kid asshole! So he's weird, well you're always stoned, so you're fucking weird by choice!

Well, *he is weird*, just like your whole dammed family. But go on baby, tell me how fucking stupid I am and how smart you are. C'mon college girl, tell me for the one thousandth time how my stoned ass would be in a coal mine somewhere in W-V-A if I wouldn't have knocked up and married the all mighty queen of Pike County . . . *little miss fuckin Ohio.*

Kit you are just a prick, a five-year-old little boy isn't going to do the things we have just watched him do for no reason, this isn't made up Kit. We just do not understand what he is seeing or trying to explain he's seen. So for once can we just be fair Kit . . . please?

Never heard of a fair prick. Fair, hmmm. Okay . . . let's see . . . Maybe there's a bum camping in our field.

Linds, for the final time, we are standing in a field looking for someone who isn't here. I'm tired of this shit woman. I'm tired of living, worrying about all of David's weird shit every fucking day of my life. Wakin up at all hours knowing that he's just standing there staring at me and then this crazy shit, well fuck . . . I'm losin it, just losin it. Oh, and you know he killed that puppy God dammit!

Lindsey with David in tow head to her Mom and Dad's house a few miles away. David is still trying to explain the man.

Hours pass and Kit knows that right or wrong he will have to patch this up somehow, so he also heads over to his in-laws to get it over with.

Lindsey's dad Russ is eating dinner on the front porch swing when Kit pulls in.

What-a-ya know boy?

Not much, Pop, not much.

Yeah Linds told me about the situation and I understand the confusion.

There's some fish and fries in the oven, oh and some sweet rolls on top, go get yerself a plate.

While leaning over to get in the oven Kit makes eye contact with Lindsey and silently mouths "I'm sorry" and she quickly and reluctantly smiles. Her expression quickly returns to the pissed look she had when Kit walked in. Kit loads up a plate and heads back out to the front porch.

Russ, I just don't know what in the hell would make a boy come up with this shit, I don't know why he would lie to us like this.

While chewing Russ stops Kit short and says, well . . . I don't think he is lying, I just don't think so.

Nearly choking, Kit responds ohhh Russ, pulease…

Now hear me out son, hear me out. Maybe your just not seeing what he sees.

What do you mean?

What I mean is that you need to look a little harder before you get so mad and accuse the boy of lying or god forbid hallucinating, look from his viewpoint and not yours. I have witnessed some odd things in this area Kit, some things I will never be able to explain.

Now, I am not telling you how to raise your child, but . . .

Just then Kit tosses the plate on the porch and leaves bitching under his breath stomping to his old truck. Russ watches him go and heads into the house.

Lindsey, you and David stay here tonight. Kit's in bad form, he'll be better tomorrow.

Russ remembers an incident with Lindsey when she was a little girl. He remembers what a hot head he could be.

Kit arrives home and plays out the entire situation over and over again. He gets close to the spot where David said that he saw the man. He gets on his knees and crawls so that he is about the same height as David. He stays this way for a very long time and sees absolutely nothing.

Kit decides that he will do this every single day to prove to Lindsey that David is either lying or hallucinating.

So day after day, and night after night Kit gets stoned and performs this ritual. He goes to exactly the spot where David said he saw the man.

Every day he becomes even more foul, Kit is starting to hate his life and all of those around him, a kind word was not spoken. Lindsey's family had never been kind to Kit, and they weren't about to start now.

Lindsey and David slowly move in with her parents. At first they stayed a night here and there, but it wasn't long before they were there all of the time.

Kit allows weeks to pass by with no communication at all with his wife and son. Lindsey is hurt, but after a while she is glad that she is separated from Kit and that she and David had moved in her parents.

After many weeks of seeing nothing, Kit is beginning to question normal everyday things, he is barely going to work and he hasn't even mowed the yard for so long the house looks abandoned.

Everyone in the area knows that they are witnessing the sad ending of a young marriage, but they could have no idea why, no one really knew.

People slowed down to look at the once well-kept little house just a few months earlier, only to see a worn path through the weeds and occasionally witnessing a very tattered looking Kit Peterson screaming profanities and flipping off any passersby for noticing.

Almost four months have now passed and Lindsey has filed for divorce. Kit accepted the papers and had never even looked through them.

It's almost Winter and all of the leaves have fallen. It's starting to get cold.

Kit is barely communicating with anyone. He has slipped into a mental state so severe that he lacks the ability to fully describe his own thoughts to himself. When he speaks he sometimes thinks he is hearing someone that he doesn't know. He walks through the house all day and all night, barely sleeping but always barely awake. His life is now resigned to a series of daily rituals performed without thinking about the reason.

Kit is unable to question his own actions. The word "why" has went missing from his existence.

Winter in southern Ohio is dammed near miserable. It doesn't always snow very much but the sky becomes and stays a depressing shade of gray for about three months straight. When you get up, it's dark, when you eat dinner, it's dark, the rest of the time it's just gray.

When the sun does show itself for a day it seems so bright and so out of place that you just can't appreciate it.

Kit heads out to the field. Everything is frosted white from a hard overnight freeze. All of the trees are bare and the grass is brown. It is sixteen degrees and he is shivering cold. He looks damn near ten years older than he is, and if he were walking with a tattered bag along Ohio Route 50, he would not look out of place.

He gets on his knees as usual and starts to inch forward so he is close to David's height. And as usual, nothing comes into view. He cups his hands together and blows into them. He stays as still as a statue for nearly 40 minutes. Watching Kit, it is very obvious that this man has fallen so far, he stares into the pasture without emotion or expression. This situation has taken a great toll while only providing misery.

Proving to Lindsey that David didn't see anything had somehow become more important than taking care of David and Lindsey or even himself.

Finally nearly frozen stiff, he starts to stand again but through the steam of the breath coming from his hands he slowly focuses on a flash at something just above the ground at what appeared to be about two or three hundred feet ahead in a large thicket.

Kit runs to the area and when he gets there he immediately loses all of the breath remaining in his lungs, he is rattled, shaking uncontrollably and almost unable to move.

Unknown to Kit, Russ had watched the first half of this event from the back of the house; he now knows for sure that Kit has lost his mind. He watched Kit crawl back and forth, tilt his head in unusual ways and do things that a normal man would not do on a sixteen degree morning kneeling in a field in southern Ohio.

A fleeting glimpse is always worth a million words, a fleeting glimpse Russ would not be afforded. Russ walked home, depressed and upset. Fairness is never popular.

Many unaccounted hours had passed. Finally back at the house Kit looked down in the large bucket that David brought back from his excavations months earlier.

He picks up and looks at a large heavily corroded aluminum emblem embossed with the name "Prairie Schooner," several metal buttons and a bottle opener on a chain.

Kit grabbed a flashlight and ran back in to the field again. He was beside himself. What had happened here? Who were these people? How could this be explained? He had to see and talk to David.

He quickly made some notes and crudely tried to draw everything he had seen on a piece of paper. Maybe Russ would understand this.

At 5:30 a.m. in the morning the phone rang at Lindseys' folks and she answered. Kit was hysteric, crying and screaming. "You need to come home now, RIGHT NOW." Russ was listening in on the other phone in the kitchen while holding his hand on the mouthpiece staring at Lindsey and shaking his head NO. It didn't matter because Lindsey was having none of it. She had been staying at her parents for months; she hung up without saying a word.

Kit hopped in his truck and sped off to Lindsey's parents. He was in a state of shock.

Normally he poked along everywhere he went, but today he was driving like a mad man. He wasn't two miles down the road when he crested a hill and ran into the back corner of a stalled flatbed truck parked halfway in the road that was overloaded with wet straw.

He was ejected through the windshield and his legs hit the dash and wheel on exit, both of them snapping like fresh picked white half-runner's.

He hit the ground tumbling through small trees and over rocks, with dirt and grass flying, all without any control or say. This happened in just a few seconds, but Kit's mind slowed down time and all of what was happening long enough for vividly clear thoughts to be present.

Time slowed so much that a few seconds seemed like a few minutes. He could smell the half frozen ground and it smelled good. He could feel moisture on his forehead and taste the frost on the grass and weeds as his face would smear into the ground during the erratic gyrations of his body.

A recurring dream he had for years, again crept in to his mind. The last two men on earth were at battle with each other.

As one of the men ran a fatal sword through the other, the mortally wounded man looked up and reached his hand toward his killer and said: *I love you*, to the very last of his fellow men that would ever be alive on the planet.

Kit now understood that dream and it brought peace upon him. He smiled one final time, he thought of Lindsey and how pretty she was. He thought of his only child David, and he dreaded what was to come.

His broken up body came to rest hanging sideways, almost upside down entangled in a fence. Every part of his body was twisted in unnatural ways and his head bobbed with each pulse of his heart.

His truck was still running and his stereo was blaring Led Zeppelin - *Battle of Evermore*. It echoed loudly through the valley.

He was in agony; he incoherently spoke in a language no one could understand.

An elderly Amish man came upon the carnage and stopped his buggy. He sat on the ground next to Kit and watched him die, realizing no aid could be rendered. His horse was uneasy and stomped back and forth due to the stress. For nearly thirty minutes Kit struggled to remain in his body, finally he departed.

All he had witnessed was lost, except for the crude sketch and notes he stuffed in his pocket.

Later in the afternoon in a totally silent and dimly lit kitchen, the Amish man's wife walked across the kitchen and slowly placed her hand on his back and asked him what was troubling him.

The man was very upset and nearly crying, he said to his wife in a strained and high pitched voice: The young English boy came out of der fast machine und he was so mangled there was no hand I could hold, und no ear to speak to.

Strange, sounds come out from his machine's radio, sounds and voices that scared me and made me have thoughts of the end times. So I set right up close to him und hold his thumb, he became still und looked in my eye. Finally by der grace of God Almighty he was taken.

All the while, Esh was uneasy, stomping back und fort. I have prayed to the all mighty to forget this day.

At this the man and his wife just sat there and looked at each other as he sobbed.

Lindsey was overcome with emotions, emotions that she could not adequately define.

She was angry and she wanted to be mad at Kit. They had been separated for months and Kit hadn't made one attempt to see their son.

At this point, she had no idea of what would unfold in her life. Nothing in this life is worse than regret.

David seemed unaffected.

A small funeral was held.

Lindsey with help from her Mom and Dad had cleaned up her house. Russ had spent several days cleaning up the yard.

David was only allowed to play in the front yard and the house.

Fall 1982 – Summer 1984

Kit had been dead for almost a year. Lindsey finally decided that she would look at the folded up piece of paper that was in Kit's pants when he died. She had always assumed it was a note to her, perhaps some explanation of why things had gone so wrong. She had thought about reading it many times but could never muster the courage to unfold it, leaving it as it was just seemed easier.

She told herself that when the time was right she would read it.

As she unfolded the paper Lindsey was devastated, it was not at all what she had expected. Instead she discovered that Kit had written a strange and ominous note:

"David is very sick, dead mummified corpses in old half buried cop car with his toys. I need help. Please come home now, I am sorry."

If Kit couldn't get his wife or in-laws to open the door, he had obviously planned on leaving the note on their door.

Kit's drawing was almost a map of their property and on this illustration he had drawn a car and labeled it "old cop car." It was at the farthest south-east corner.

He had described finding the car by seeing a "flash" that came from the sun reflecting off the remaining chrome and glass of a large spotlight mounted on the driver's side of the car.

Lindsey immediately called her father Russ.

Lindsey and her Father made their way back to where David had been digging a year earlier, as they made their way into the thicket, both were in a state of shock.

Exposed to the light of day for the first time in over 30 years, was the top and side of a late 1940s police car, with most everything still intact. It was amazingly well preserved as it had been buried in sandy loam soil.

The car contained two well preserved mummified corpses.

David had placed toys all around them and had put hats on them. He had drawn pictures for them. It was an awful scene with horrific implications.

Russ immediately knew where the old police cruiser came from, and so did Jenny. Russ knew that it would be almost impossible to see any part of the car during the spring and summer months with all of the leaves on, as the dense thicket encircled the entire site. How the half buried Sheriff's car could have been overlooked for over 30 years was easy to understand, no one cared. The work to clear the area would have never been worth the land underneath.

Russ called the Sheriff, the Sheriff called the State Patrol and the State Patrol called the FBI.

What David had discovered was a 30-year-old mystery, but it was even more of a mystery than anyone could imagine.

Russ was a young man when all of this happened and his father-in-law and first cousin were lying in the back of that police car. Jenny was confused and sick. She had always figured that her father had been murdered over the beer and cigarette racket, never to be found alive.

Cops don't up and vanish like a fart in the wind, especially in Southern Ohio in the early 1950s. When that actually happened it was a scandal, with public outrage, hell it made national news. It put fear into people beyond compare; it stressed an area of southern Ohio like it had never been stressed. Everyone from the Feds to aliens were blamed. Rumors raged on for years.

Only two would ever know the actual truth and they had been lying in each other's laps for dammed near 32 years in the back of a police car buried in a field.

As the car was fully unearthed, news teams from across the US were assembled at the entrance to the Peterson property. Helicopters were flying overhead, it was a circus. A load of beer and cigarettes were discovered in the trunk. The well preserved mummified remains of two bodies were found lying across each other in the back seat. Even their clothing was in remarkable condition.

Russ and Jenny are visited by the FBI, the corpses in the police car have been positively identified. They are Sheriff Charlie Gifford and Leon Robarts. A crime is suspected, but it will remain under investigation for decades.

Jenny is inconsolable. She explains that Leon Robarts had a long-term affair with her mother and that Sheriff Gifford was her father. She was never questioned when her father went missing. She was too embarrassed and ashamed to ever discuss her mother's unusual behavior and her mother's affair with Leon.

Amazingly they also discovered the land they had helped Kit and Lindsey purchase was once owned by Birch Robarts who was Lindsey's grandfather and Russ's biological father.

Jenny tells the agent about her Sheriff father's involvement in the illegal beer sales many years ago.

The situation for Lindsey was now almost unthinkable. How could David have possibly thought this was normal? Why he hadn't described more of what he had seen was beyond disturbing.

David and Lindsey would go through an intensive eight month therapy program, driving to Columbus twice a week. The psychiatrist asked Lindsey if there was anyone else in the family that she knew of who had suffered from mental illnesses, she answered no, but told the doctor that she wasn't sure about David's father's side of the family.

Lindsey was completely unaware of David's great-grandmother Janet, his great grandfathers, Charlie and Birch, great-great Aunt Elizabeth and most of all his first cousin twice removed, Leon.

The doctor reviews the entire situation with Lindsey:

Lindsey, mental illness isn't often recognized and many times it is not discussed even if known because people are ashamed of themselves or their relative's deeds and/or their life. The havoc that inherited mental illness reeks in our society is in my estimate, massive. Many studies including brain scans are now serving as proof of the genetic links involved in mental illness. At least by those who will accept the sound science which conclusively proves it.

We must be acutely aware of past relatives who have suffered child abuse, *Birch, Elizabeth, Leon* committed murder (especially at an early age) *Birch,* committed rape (again especially at an early age) *Leon,* committed suicide *Sheriff Gifford,* or had an unusual and/or overcharged sex life with multiple partners, etc. *Leon, Janet Gifford.* Also, relatives who lived withdrawn lives, etc. *Kit, Birch, Leon, Sheriff Gifford.*

All of the aforementioned behaviors are red flashing lights, warnings for us to watch for symptoms/behaviors in our own lives and the lives of our children. They are the direct indicators we can pinpoint for mental illness with familial connections. There doesn't have to be a genetic component, but in David's situation, I strongly believe there is, albeit unknown to you.

As well, many times in today's society parents with mentally ill children inadvertently try to make excuses for unusual behaviors. This delays the potential of an accurate diagnosis, and quite possibly exposes civil society to a murderer, rapist, even God forbid, a politician or president, all depending on when and if diagnosis is made, if treatment begins, and if that treatment proves to be effective.

If it is a young child who is mentally ill, one parent often ends up being a life-long "co-dependent defender" of a child's unusual behaviors. This can lead to marital issues, divorce etc. This co-dependency can be incredibly strong and very dangerous.

You should also be aware of how the psychopath with narcissistic tendencies views right and wrong.

Wrong in word or deed can only happen to them, in other words, only "they" can be wronged, no one else. *Right* is everything they do regardless of the outcome, period. I realize this may be tricky to understand, but this is how their minds function.

Also, they can be off the chart brilliant, cunning, and highly successful. Or at the other end of the spectrum they can be downtrodden and remain that way all of their life. It is truly the genetic lottery in all regards. These children disregard the passing of time all of their lives. They may recall an incident that occurred twenty years earlier, acting as if it were just five minutes ago. The passing of time does not diminish or enhance their emotions concerning an event long passed and forgotten by most.

I am personally aware of a co-dependent mother who helped her adult son bury his murder victim, being so drawn in that she completely disregarded the fact she was burying a dead human being. Her son then exhumed the body acting as if he was communicating with the corpse.

The mother then re-buried the corpse in a different location where her son could not exhume the body again, thus infuriating the son to the point that he then killed his own mother. I will not discuss his disposition with her corpse. My point to you Lindsey is that co-dependencies can be quite insidious and highly volatile as mentally ill children grow to become adults, even lethal.

As they grow into adults, a small percentage of these children become capable of horrific crimes, even after years of seemingly passive behavior. They are truly like a light switch and there are few if any warning signs.

Recalling all of David's childhood to this point, everything suddenly becomes painfully obvious, it's as if a fog has lifted, a terribly tragic fog based only on that which she is aware of. Breaking down to the point that she hyperventilates and nearly passes out, Lindsey is swirling in a sea of absolute misery. Reality has become a very cruel and permanent host.

One thing is now certain, minute by minute, day by day, David is incapable of understanding, controlling or predicting his own actions, and so is his co-dependent mother.

David will forever be incapable of matching his physical expressions with the emotions he wants to portray.

Completely unknown to Lindsey, are the lives and behaviors of her deceased family members who will continue their relentless genetic haunt until not a trace of the bloodline remains. It's as if David is pulling a log chain attached to a kite of each of his mentally ill family members floating behind him in the blackness of space. All of them having a direct pathway to his mind, like one way conduits transporting heinous requests at the cellular level, easily satisfied with their genetic host's unexplained actions in the physical world where physical time applies, where now is truly now as best we can define it. No one ever realizing what is truly going on behind the scenes transcending space and time. These people are truly clairvoyant, they have the ability to see, hear and mimic the future and the past with absolute clarity, never separating one from the other.

Lindsey listens to a scientific theorist discussing mental illness…

It's at the quantum level, it always has been. It is truly HELL, it is where Satan exists if he exists at all. Mentally ill people aren't just mentally ill, they are plugged into a horrific world that we are not, where quantum events are not distinguished past from present, where now is forever now and what has happened is just happening because it happened, where events are continuously taking place so blazingly fast and so microscopically small that they cannot be witnessed with the current resolution of the technology we are now studying these events with. The sequence of these events seemingly irrelevant until a "matched" without obvious reason organic/biological host comes into cue, at that point the sequence never mattering more.

Soon, we will make medical advancements at the subatomic level that will be so unreal; they will initially not be believed. Even the researchers will be unable to put into perspective the scope of their new discoveries. Where there is a front door, there is a back door and a side door and a door within each door, within each door. Etc. What we can't see, is affecting everything we can see more than anyone currently understands.

But for now we wait, unable to predict the actions of the mentally ill as they are unable to provide any logical reasons for those actions. You may never know your forefathers, but one thing is certain, on a cellular level they will know you.

David was diagnosed as a severe schizophrenic psychopath. He had hallucinations; he lacked the ability to fully realize life or death. David had insisted that the corpses of his unknown great-grandfather and cousin played with him and talked to him. He calmly explained to a therapist as he had to his mother that "they" had not "walked into the other room."

Then there was the puppy incident.

The psychiatrist told Lindsey that David made little distinction between life and death. He could not understand that his own existence or anyone's existence was a biological one, that his body was an organic body. David did not comprehend what a lifespan would be. He was not able to accurately distinguish the gender of himself or others.

He *would always be this way*; he had always been this way.

Kit was right all along, David did need to see a doctor. Knowing that he had at least partially understood this catastrophe while having no one who would listen, and that he had died rushing to inform her, hurt Lindsey so much that she would never forgive herself. She will now anguish forever the fact that it was not Kit who abandoned his family; it was his family at her insistence who abandoned him.

Lindsey reflects on her life. She cannot begin to describe her feelings, or define the depth of her misery. She is devastated that her son is mentally ill and would always be. That he had played with the corpses of her grandfather and cousin. She could not believe that they had somehow purchased the land where these people were buried. She missed Kit and she would forever regret not talking to him on the phone. David remained unaffected.

Summer 1984

For the first time in almost two years, David was allowed to again play in the field. Lindsey was relieved. While things would never be the same, it was time to move forward with life. After intensive counseling, their day to day existence had become more settled.

David takes his many prescribed medications. He has reluctantly learned to tell time, although he despises being asked by his mother what time it is.

She confidently watches him from the back of the house. David slowly walks to the far corner of the field abruptly stops and begins to slowly inch back and forth.

Lindsey stares at him in complete silence for several minutes. He then rapidly plops down almost falling on the ground. Lindsey can just see the top of David's head moving back and forth over the tall grass and weeds.

She screams his name as she walks and then runs towards him, he gets up and slowly walks toward his approaching mother. *David is looking only straight up.... with only the whites of his eyes visible.*

Lindsey is nearly frozen in fear and very out of breath but she reluctantly asks, David . . . David . . . what is going on David . . . what are you doing?

Mommy, the man lays he's head on my legs and looks at me.

What man David?

The man in the field that asks for you Mommy.

What man asks for me David?

David is turning in slow circles looking straight up in the sky. Again Lindsey loudly asks, David, there is a man who asks for me?

Yes, it's my Dad, do you remember Kit?

Lindsey's mouth involuntarily opens completely, she looks at David in absolute and complete terror, she drops to the ground on her knees unable to speak or cry, gasping for breath she tries to crawl but she is unable to move. David stands next to her and looks at her and then looks up at the crow circling high above, he appears unaffected.

An Understanding of Sorts May 2009

When the FBI agents walk into Violet's apartment, they cannot comprehend what they are hearing and seeing. It defies all explanation.

Violet's entire living space is a work of art. It is a large white space with a low angled white ceiling, bright lighting, white walls, white floor, with life-sized cutout pictures of Hugh and Ursal mounted on white boards. Multiple computer generated voices played in odd pitches and tones, praying as the boys did, saying the same thing over and over, computer generated voices requesting horrible things . . .

You know, Vi says, "computer generated voices requesting things in unison can affect the biological outcomes of some situations."

Madam are we not here for your "art" exhibit, we are here to seeking information about Hugh, the special needs child that you adopted in the 1940s. Violet tells the agents that he lives outside of Athens, Ohio in a mental health facility.

The agents comment to each other about this woman who has to be in her eighties, looks and acts like she is in her fifties.

A week later a FBI agent arrives in southern Ohio. He watches Hugh with binoculars from two buildings away. As he watches, he phones in to report. I can tell you, this is going to be just as bizarre as the Chicago visit, I am heading in for a chat.

As he hangs up he notices Hugh looking back at him through a telescope, Hugh waves and gestures at the agent, flipping him off.

The agent heads into the facility to talk with Hugh. With his unusually high pitched raspy voice and his flamboyant appearance, Hugh greets the agent at the door to his room.

With a battered fur stole wrapped around his neck, wearing ladies horned-rimmed glasses from the 1940s and an overabundance of make-up, Hugh is going bald with just a few long tufts of hair in every direction. He has only a few remaining teeth.

The agent asks Hugh about his life and he listens in absolute disbelief as Hugh recollects. He tells the agent that his real father was Leon Robarts and his real mother was Diana Smith.

Let's see, let me see here . . . Yep, I got some stuff to tell you.

Well, first we was with the preacher, and he was a bastard, just a crazy prick. Locked us in the cellar, but we prayed for him to die. Then Mame bought us from the preacher.

Mame and Daddy sued the preacher for chopping our nuts off. Crazy ain't it, I am a no-balled man! *No marbles in the old sack, but I don't take it in the crack! Pocket pool is not my game!*

Hugh was laughing so hard that he takes a minute to catch himself. The agent is stunned and sets there without comment, mouth open.

Hugh continues:

Then the preacher got kicked out of town and his boy Paul killed him by stickin a screwdriver in the back of his neck while he was preachin' at a campground, peddlin mis-printed versions of the King James from his trunk. He always made Paul dig em out of the burn barrels at the Bible printers *(a workin for a jeeezus!)*. Then on the same day, Paul went to meet the Lord in person. Yep, he up and hopped right off a bridge over the Ohio river, but he couldn't swim and the water was too far down. So you know, SPLAT, glug, glug, glug. Hugh holds his nose and acts like he is drowning, waving his arm with his eyes closed.

Me and my brother almost burned our house down at the hot water tank looking at naked girls with giant pointy boobs, like really big fat pointy naked tits, God I love um. Don't you love um? In the 40s and 50s tits were pointy. But tits ain't pointy anymore, and it seriously bothers me. *But we got WAY bigger fish to fry here ain't we? . . . Hugh laughed.*

Let's see . . .

Then... the old artist queer on the hill, kicked the bucket and his Chinese gurlfriend "a-hem" who was really a boy by the name of Marion, *(Hugh rolls his eyes)* gave Mame and Daddy the big house and a drawer full of money.

Then Daddy shot himself in the face because he robbed this bank, but he really didn't, anyhow he still died in the barn.

Then Mame took in a group of really goofy lookin kids for us to teach um manners. But me and Ursal, we taught um birds and bees. Hugh chuckled, we taught um who was girls and who was boys and what the difference was. Those goofy kids would play "hide the pee pee" games all night, and they loved it! We really loved it too...if you get my drift.

After that my brother got beat to death for practicin bein a gurl, and Mame got kicked out of high in the middle and round on both ends o-HI-o, and moved back to Chicago, and she ain't been allowed to talk with me since but she still does. Someday I'm going to visit her. I miss Mame.

Finally, I ended up at this fuckin five star . . . ah, foo foo tah tah "<u>Resort Lodge,</u>" listening to all the crazy fuckers make weird sounds all day and night while they shit themselves and then do artwork with their own poop! . . . Great ain't it? Want a menu? May I suggest the Salisbury steak, with institutional gravy over whipped potatoes and corn? All combined it makes great abstract wall art before or after indigestion!

The now speechless agent asks about Hugh's friend David Peterson down the hall.

He's crazier than fuck! I mean off the chart nuts. Hugh spins his finger next to his head and crosses his eyes. He dug up my daddy and his great grand pappy in a field. See, my daddy was his cousin, but my daddy wasn't related to his grand pappy, so, . . . well never mind it's confusing . . . then his daddy got killed flying out of his truck.

But the best thing is that my real Daddy did fuck his Great-Grammy, pretty God dammed funny ain't it? My Daddy *(Hugh sticking his finger in the loop of his opposite hand)* fucking his Great-Grammy!

At Christmas time, I made up a little song for him:

My daddy fucked yer great-gramaw, fucked her up the ass on Christmas Eve . . ., you can't say there's no such thing as . . .

The agent just sits there in complete amazement as Hugh sings his vulgar rendition of the Christmas favorite.

Oh yeah, and my real Mommy, her name was Diana. Well, she was from Prince, West Virginia and she was Kit Peterson's, (you know David's dad who's dead) well she was his aunt. Yep, Kit's mother's family got broke up after a mine accident. So his mom and her two brother's went to live at a cousins in Beckley, but nobody wanted my mom (Diana) cause she was a little retarded and older, so she ended up at an orphanage in Ohio and then all over the place. Hell we're kin from both sides of the fence, second cousins twice and one half removed!

Hugh tells the agent not to waste his time talking to David.

He tells the agent, David says that he sees things, you know like ghosts, spirits, I guess even Santy fuckin Claus! But it's all just bullshit. Hugh goes on, but he sings dammed good, crazy fucker, but he sings real good.

As the agent leaves, he is astonished at the oddities of the area and the people involved. He drives to the nearest bar, turns off his cell phone and sets in the corner while trying to put the day into some sort of perspective.

Hugh hobbles into his wheelchair to visit David Peterson who lives three rooms down the hall. David turned 33 today. He has been in the home with Hugh since 1984. His mother Lindsey visits him once a month. Hugh watches as she leaves.

David received an iPod for his birthday from his mother. It is loaded with his favorite music. He listens repeatedly to Bad Company, knowing it was one of his father's favorite bands.

David offers Hugh one of his ear buds and they sit very close while listening. He is a better friend than Hugh would ever admit.

David sings so spot on and so beautifully to the song "Ready for Love" while Hugh with eyes closed, gently rocks back and forth to the music and David's lovely voice. He can be heard throughout the facility, even two floors up. It silences almost everyone.

Lindsey arrives home, to the same home she purchased with Kit many years ago.

Everything is the same. Nothing has changed. Her father Russ is getting old and has a hard time getting around. He has made a few trips to the hospital lately.

She walks out to the field every day and sometimes at night looking and begging for an understanding she will never receive.

Case Wrap Up, June 2, 2009

The special agent assigned to the case notices the director he reports to rubbing his arm.

FBI Agent:

Is something wrong with your arm sir?

FBI Director:

I don't know, I have a pinching sensation at the shoulder. Muscle spasm.

FBI Agent:

Do you have any aspirins sir?

FBI Director:

I can't take them, they give me nose bleeds. The hell with my arm, let's get this show on the road.

Finally the FBI summarizes (agent to investigation director) what they have assembled:

FBI Agent:

Okay we have known each other for many years correct . . .

FBI Director:

Yes…

FBI Agent:

Well then . . . here we go. In 1981…

FBI Director:

Stop. Why 1981?

FBI Agent:

Fuck if I know, seemed like a good place to start. Please bear with me sir, this is complex.

FBI Director:

Uh okay, continue…

FBI Agent:

In 1981 David Peterson claims to have seen some type of an apparition of his maternal great grandfather (Sheriff Charlie Gifford), although he didn't know who he was at the time, he also digs.

FBI Director:

Stop. So the Peterson boy . . . uh . . . David, claims that he sees an apparition of his dead maternal great grandfather, and doesn't know it's his great grandfather?

FBI Agent:

Correct. If I may continue sir, by digging up the police cruiser, he (David Peterson) then also partially exhumes the grave of his maternal great grandfather (Sheriff Charlie Gifford), and his paternal first cousin twice removed (Leon Robarts), who had an affair with his great grandmother (Janet Gifford). They all died before they were related to David, obviously before he was born. Leon Robarts was never related to the Giffords.

Also, in 1981 just prior to the aforementioned events, Lindsey Peterson and her now long dead husband Kit purchased the land that her maternal grandfather (Sheriff Charlie Gifford) was buried on.

This land was once owned by her paternal grandfather (Birch Robarts) at the time her maternal grandfather (Sheriff Charlie Gifford), went missing.

A defect on the property deed and corresponding tax records never listed Birch Robarts as the owner even though he purchased the tract at the same time and from the same seller as his other property.

Lindsey Peterson's paternal grandfather (Birch Robarts) died of a heart attack the same day that her maternal grandfather (Sheriff Charlie Gifford) went missing/died, and on the same day that her grandmother's lover (Leon Robarts), her first cousin once removed, went missing-died. All dates were more or less confirmed by forensics.

FBI Director:

Un-fucking real, I cannot believe this shit, and none of these people were related or anything when this happened?

FBI Agent:

Correct. Also in 1981 Kit Peterson died rushing over to his estranged wife's parents to tell her that he had found where their son David had been digging and to tell her that there was a partially unearthed police car in their field that had two bodies in the back that David had tried to play with.

FBI Director:

How do we know that?

FBI Agent:

Because of the note his wife was given that was removed from his trousers while preparing the corpse for burial.

FBI Director:

This is the craziest of all shit I have ever had to deal with in my entire career. Are we missing anything in this unbelievable cluster fuck? Is this it?

FBI Agent:

Hardly. The surviving twin we spoke with in Athens, Ohio who was adopted from a church by Mrs. Hoffmiller and her long ago deceased husband Bernard, claimed that his biological father was (Leon Robarts) who was corpse number two found in the cruiser on the Peterson land. Forensics has now confirmed this as fact. Also, his mother Diana Smith, who by some accounts was basically murdered by Leon Robarts, was Kit Peterson's aunt. Diana Smith was Kit Peterson's mothers' oldest sibling. The family was separated after a mining accident.

FBI Director:

Jesus, so the crazy fucking handicapped guy who is in the state run nut house in Athens, Ohio with the fur stole and horned brimmed glasses and the uh uh . . . makeup and all that shit, is the surviving son of Leon Robarts, the man who killed the Sheriff because he was fucking the Sheriffs wife?

FBI Agent:

Surviving son yes, killer of the Sheriff no, forensics has determined that the Sheriff killed himself.

FBI Director:

So . . . Let me understand . . . Leon Robarts was fucking the Sheriffs wife . . . but Leon Robarts didn't kill the Sheriff and Leon Robarts didn't kill himself, *but by a weird coincidence they somehow end up as dead BFFs in the backseat of the sheriff's cruiser buried in the field of his* **NOW,** *but not then grand-daughter for over 30 years together?*

FBI Agent:

Dead BFFs yes, coincidence yes, grand-daughter yes, but . . . again NO, Leon Robarts didn't Kill Sheriff Gifford.

FBI Director:

What . . . the . . . fuck, so someone else killed Leon Robarts?

FBI Agent:

Yes.

FBI Director:

Who?

FBI Agent:

We uh . . . we are still working on that sir. Forensics has determined that Leon Robarts was shot in the top of the head by a third party with the same gun the Sheriff used to kill himself. It is impossible to shoot yourself in the top of the head at the angle he was shot at.

FBI Director:

Well for fuck sake, will you please shoot me in the top of the head, please? Stop working on it. This shit could just not be made up. I have never heard of a situation spanning over 50 years with so many overlapping or partially overlapping incidents of what we call *relatives in common*. It's just a God dammed disaster, these people should have stopped breeding generations ago! All of this because one dead guys son married another dead guy's daughter. What a crazy mess.

FBI agent:

But sir, if I may, do these men who were buried in a field or their families not deserve for the story of their demise to be understood or told?

FBI Director:

Please . . . , their surviving families . . . well . . . this is a long-term nightmare for them. A crazy little kid trying to play with the corpse or corpses or whatever the, you know . . . multiple . . . you know the two dead people, then his parents separate, then as a little kid David's father tragically dies. And now, he is thirty some years old and in the very same nut house with his cousin, the old transvestite lunatic . . . then all of the media. At this point, no one really gives a shit.

FBI Agent:

But sir is it not important to figure out at least the relationships between the deceased and their families, if nothing else to prevent the potential of intermarriage?

FBI Director:

Intermarriage? (the director is laughing) Are YOU fucking kidding me? Intermarriage? This is southern Ohio, being related is not a deterrent to marriage, these people arrange marriages at family picnics, in fact, well never mind. Drop it, just drop it.

As the director is gazing out of his window he wonders how in the hell all of this could have happened. It's Friday afternoon and he is going to tee off bright and early and 8 a.m. The reality of this situation is becoming very clear and that is it doesn't really matter who killed who. No one will believe the story no matter who tells it, in no way can this situation be cleaned up at least not cleaned up enough for anyone to make any sense of it.

At 4:01 a.m. on Saturday morning, the FBI Director dies of a massive heart attack. He never wakes, up. As the alarm goes off at 7:20 a.m., his wife screams in complete agony as she realizes that her hard as a rock husband has silently died right beside her as they slept.

With three carts full of impatient government lard insisting they begin, and twenty cell phones blaring with stupid digital renditions of 60s and 70s songs, (one of them playing Led Zepplin – Battle of Evermore) his pals decide that he can catch up with them and they tee off at exactly 8:05 a.m. Saturday morning. Because as the director said: "No one really gives a shit."

Chapter 12, Hello 2012

Three years later.

It's an early Saturday morning outside of Waverly, Ohio, only a few days until the end of October. The sodium lamp over the garage flickered its final time years earlier. The typical Appalachia fog has rolled in. The unmistakable stench of the pulp yard has drifted south, carrying with it the aroma of sour rotting apples on the ground, campfires and burn barrels. The familiar scents of all that is dying or dead. All of the smells from autumn mixed together in a recollecting concoction. Pumpkins, Indian corn and gourds of all shapes and sizes now reside on front porches. A gentle fall rain had insured that everything not under roof was glassy wet and drenched completely.

Lindsey Peterson had drifted off to sleep hours earlier, dreaming of days past when life seemed to matter more, a time when the complexities of life had not yet closed in on her. Now 53 years old, she wonders where her life has gone, she remembers meeting Kit and coaxing him to dance with her at the Mosquito Dam Jam. Her father Russ had died a few years earlier and she missed him terribly. She missed his voice, and the advice he would offer. She remembered being a little girl watching cartoons with him on Saturday morning, as he would cook sourdough pancakes.

Russ had been the first and only remaining man in her life, her go to person when life was shit, the first to congratulate her when there was any reason to, and the one who could console her when the pains of life were too great.

At one minute past four o'clock in the morning, Lindsey is startled as she sets up in bed, her heart racing, beating in her throat. It sounds like someone is trying to beat her front door down.

Rattle, rattle, rattle . . . Knock, knock, . . . THUD, THUD, THUD…

There are emergency lights flashing through the curtains on her wall and ceiling. She quickly gets out of bed and looks out the window only to see a Sheriff's cruiser with lights on sitting half-way up her gravel lane.

The cruiser looks wrecked; steam is pouring out from under the hood. The Sheriff is sitting with his door open looking toward the house. This can't be good, something must be wrong.

Grabbing her robe, preparing to run down the lane, she is completely shocked, frozen mid step as she opens the door. . . David is standing in the doorway.

He is covered from head to toe in blood, puke and feces. He has a bloody bottle opener sticking out of his pocket with a chain running off of it attached to his belt loop. His pants are partially unzipped and unbuttoned with long strips of bloody skin hanging from his half zipped fly.

He has the Sheriff's gun belt draped across his shoulder (with the gun still in the open holster) and his iPod is in his shirt pocket with his ear buds in.

David had not been to his childhood home for over thirty years. *He is looking straight up with only the whites of his eyes visible, his eyes fluttering rapidly. He will not look at his mother.*

Lindsey is shaking uncontrollably as she tries to speak, but David beats her to the first word spoken between them.

Still looking straight up with his eyes fluttering and his mouth is moving in unusual ways, David is obviously having a hard time speaking.

Finally David asks with a high pitched stutter: "la la Lindsey, Lindsey . . . . . . where is ch cha Charcoal? He then calmly calls for his childhood puppy . . . here ch cha Charcoal . . . . . He then suddenly screams with a loud strange voice Lindsey has never heard; "**WHERE IS MY FUCKIN PUPPY BITCH?**"

David, look at me, David . . . David what are you doing? Why are you here? Did the police bring you here?

David is still looking only straight up.... with only the whites of his eyes visible.

Yes, ye yes Lindsey, I am home . . . . . . with you . . . . . . and Kit . . . . . . and Charcoal.

David, Let's walk down and talk to the officer who brought you, please?

David's is still looking only straight up, his eyes are still fluttering and blinking wildly. He will not make eye contact.

Okay Lindsey, let's talk to *him*.

As Lindsey gets closer to the cruiser she realizes the horror that is unfolding here. The cruisers windows and interior are spattered with feces, blood, and urine. The Sheriff was only sitting there because his neck was wrapped tight to the head rest support rods with a tan colored seat belt that had been cut from the car. His body was riddled with multiple bullet wounds. He was nude and completely mutilated from the waist down.

With Lindsey gasping for air and slowly backing away, David kneels down looking at the dead Sheriff, running his fingers through his hair while he pleasantly smiles looking straight at the sheriff's corpse nose to nose as if they are young lovers.

Holding the sheriff's head tightly by his hair, David quickly twists the head of the corpse, slowly licking the murdered sheriff's face and ear as if he was licking cake icing from a spatula.

With complete calm, he erotically moans and whispers . . . . . .Oh… Oh… she is so pretty for me . . . she loves me now. . .

Looking sideways at Lindsey he asks, do you know what time it is?

David then rapidly springs up, standing fully. With a strong West Virginia accent while grinning wildly with neck stretched, David speaks loudly and perfectly with his father's voice: **"HE AIN'T LOVING ANYONE NOW GOD DAMMIT, HE'S DEADER THAN A FUCKIN DOORNAIL. WHAT DID YOU DO?"**

As David speaks, Lindsey simultaneously hears and sees Kit saying exactly the same thing after finding him pulling around the dead puppy thirty years earlier.

Without the possibility of any other thoughts or actions, this repeats in her mind over and over. Complete misery now grips her body, with the full command of David's insanity dragging her straight into an unbearable hell.

Panicking to the point of complete and uncontrolled madness, Lindsey wails helplessly, running and screaming through the yard in all directions, pleading for something she is not capable of defining.

On David's third shot with eyes fluttering he strikes her in the back from five feet away, completely shattering her spine just below the neck.

Lindsey is dead, without the luxury or curse of last thoughts. David carries her across his back skipping around the yard while hollering and giggling without smiling. He then places his mother's body in the cruiser with the sheriff, laying her in his lap.

David then stops and screams, reciting in voices from relatives past that he couldn't possibly have ever known or ever heard:

"Leon, we've got to bury this awful mess. The car and all?

Yes dumbass the car and all. First go get me some rags from the wrecker, and then start cleaning the blood off the windows."

He walks into the house, kicking the door shut behind him. David can be faintly heard through the walls and closed door singing the "Picture Pages" song from Captain Kangaroo.

The Sheriff's Cruiser continues to run, lights on, radio blaring.

Hansen, Hansen…..you there Hansen? Hansen report immediately! . . .

Hansen! .   .   .   .   .   . God dammit Hansen you respond,……… H A N S E N !

When the authorities find the atrocity the next day, David is in the back seat of the cruiser sleeping soundly. He had placed his remaining childhood toys all around the corpses of his mother and the sheriff.

David had drawn abstract faces on waxed paper and taped his artwork on to his mother and the sheriff as if they were wearing masks. The faint translucent images of the corpses underneath combined with the cartoonish drawings were so horrific that words could not define the feelings of the responding authorities.

David was calmly arrested.

Chapter 13, Goodbye My Friend

Aged and sickly, Hugh Hoffmiller sits in the same rundown state nursing facility that he has been in for decades. The old brick structure was a former high school built in the 1930s that had been converted into a mental health facility in 1975. Hugh was one of the first occupants. The halls of the old school echo with the voices of the misunderstood and completely vacant stares from those who are silent and unable to speak or respond.

Hugh, who is now barely able to walk, sobs quietly in David's empty room as he looks out of the window at a cold November rain. He looks through the old windows of the school which are now held together with only sparse chunks of dried out glazing holding the many cracked panes of glass in their rusty frames.

He stares down at the buckled and mostly missing pavement of the side parking lot of the facility, where there are more dead weeds than remaining blacktop. He remembers the secret of life that Mame said to him: "where there can be life, there will be life" and in all of his life, this has been the only thing that was true.

Hugh gets on the barely functioning old PA system and with his raspy voice, he recites a portion of the former pastor Williams favorite sermon, adding his own amens, hallehluyas and clapping:

Children of God…Ye must seek the path of righteousness, hallehluya brother, walking the path of truth….Amen, amen. I am the light, and I WILL LIFT you from darkness, do not be AFRAID, do not be ALONE…You cannot hide from the LORD . . .

The echo through the timeworn school coupled with the crackling old PA system is haunting. Hugh's sermon reached about half of the rooms in the facility. Most of the rooms had dropped tile ceilings that muffled the sound from the hidden old speakers that rested several feet above.

All of the nursing and administrative staff looked up from their tasks, rolled their eyes, and in near unison murmured, oh Jesus….Hugh is preaching on the PA again. Visitors were always the most startled, clueless as to what they were hearing and from whom.

Hugh misses his friend David, at times it is unbearable for him. He had known and lived in the same facility with his cousin for over twenty five years. David was a connection for Hugh to the only group of people he could have ever known to call family.

Hugh could not believe what David had done; he could not believe the quiet man with the most beautiful voice he had ever heard had brutally killed a sheriff and his own mother. It seemed so far from being possible.

For many years David was all that Hugh had, his only friend, the only blood relative he really ever knew, the one person who would listen. He was in fact the last living family member that Hugh would ever know.

David was the last person with whom Hugh would share *Relatives In Common*.

As sad as this day was, all was not lost for Hugh. A new adventure was about to begin, it would be Hugh's last adventure.

For the first time in many years Hugh unfolds the poem his mother Diana had written for him before he was born, he prays to her, thanking her for this life.

Smiling from ear to ear, he boards the bus bound for his new home in Chicago with Mame. He has not set the card down since receiving it.

All of the preparations had been made. Hugh would have his own nurse, his own living area and daily conversations with the only person other than Ursal who really ever cared about him in this life.

As the bus arrived in Chicago, Hugh was speechless. There were people everywhere. More people than he had ever seen, thousands of people, some smiling, some not, with thousands of destinations. It was overwhelming.

- Fade to black –